# Rumpled

# Rumpled

Lacey Louwagie

Late-night Books, Sioux Falls 57106

http://www.laceylouwagie.com

Lacey Louwagie has been writing since she was old enough to hold a pencil and fold a few pieces of paper together. Her first book, full of pictures of unicorns, started her on the path of writing science fiction and fantasy. She has worked as a freelance writer and editor, magazine editor, reporter, and librarian. She lives in a tiny house in South Dakota with her husband, two cats, a dog, and hundreds of books.

ISBN 978-0991540112

Published in Sioux Falls, South Dakota

Printed in the United States

## *To Ivan*

for asking the "what if?" question that started it all

Here's the thing about babies: they're never around when you need them. And when you don't want 'em, they're everywhere. Everyone has a story of a May princess who starts to round out like the moon as the summer closes, who cries behind her house as she feeds the chickens, because the lad she enchanted at the spring festival was betrothed to another all along.

Or there's the girl who is ill-used by her father, or her brother. People look away, pretending that it's from some boy she met secretly in alleys. But no matter how much they look away, the baby comes, and no one wants it there.

I was a baby like that. And who could blame my dear mother? Every woman dreams of a beautiful baby, ten perfectly formed fingers and toes, sparkling blue eyes, and a tiny upturned nose, perhaps a dusting of golden hair.

I had ten fingers and toes. That was something.

Laurus had never seen me as a baby, but he told me even a baby like I had been—s-shaped spine, fingers like dead twigs, a smile full of crooked teeth—would do. Laurus didn't dream of a beautiful baby. Just a baby in its first year of life.

"I'm not going to be around forever," he lamented, pushing his hood back and running his hand over his wispy gray hair. "A man with knowledge like mine needs someone to pass it on to."

"You've taught me so much."

He shook his head, his thin, pink mouth pulling his whole face into a frown. "You've been with me seven years, Rumpel, and you've only learned transmutation. You were what, fifteen, when you came to me? Already you had fifteen years of clutter in your brain. You could never have the space to learn everything I know. I need an empty receptacle into which I can pour my wisdom before it becomes lost from this world."

I didn't want it to be lost, either—not before I learned the final transmutation. And to learn it, I had to pay Laurus. I had to bring him a child in its first year of life.

Oh, I considered sneaking through windows and snatching babies where they slept. After all, it was easy enough for most people to make another. But for all Laurus could do, he could not do *that*. When I asked him why he'd never fathered children of his own, he shook his head and said, "You cannot have great power without great sacrifice."

I didn't pry further; one does not question the virility of his master.

As for me, *those* parts worked just fine, though I had scant opportunity to use them. No woman would bed me, not without the final transmutation. And I wouldn't take one against her will, for the same reason I wouldn't steal a baby under cover of night.

I didn't want my heart to become as twisted as my body.

"What if I brought you a lamb, or a kitten?" I suggested. I knew transmutation of live entities was possible, although I'd only achieved it on insects, rodents, and birds. "And then, perhaps, you could transmute it into a baby . . ."

Laurus's ice-blue eyes narrowed into slits. "Do you really believe I should bequeath all my knowledge upon a *kitten*?"

My face heated.

"I tire of gold pieces," Laurus sighed. "And you're fast approaching the limits of your abilities. Is there even anything you *want* from me, besides the final transmutation?"

I opened my mouth to reply, but Laurus continued, "No, I didn't think so. Focus your energy on procuring the child. After that, you may return for more teaching."

If I had my way, I would have made finding that damn baby my full-time job. But the world has never been in the habit of conspiring on my behalf. It cares nothing for a man with a twisted body. A man with a twisted mind, that's different. That kind of man, the world lets him be King.

I suppose it had been blessing enough, when one of the King's buyers plucked me out of an orphanage when I was thirteen, the age at which many orphans were picked up to provide childcare or farm labor. He thought King Lucas might find some amusement in me, and indeed he did. When the buyer marched me up to his throne, the King bent forward, peered at me through narrowed eyes, and then leaned back and laughed. "Why, what is this? I've never seen such a man! What can he do?"

"I might train him to do a few tricks, some dancing."

"Yes, yes, you must!" King Lucas clapped his hands and tossed back his head, his wavy brown hair swaying against his cheeks. He was nineteen then, just a boy himself, as tall and thin as a cattail, his face still too smooth for shaving. "He shall amuse my guests."

King Lucas was known for parties that boasted the best entertainment in the Seven Kingdoms, and soon I became part of it. I trained under the King's dancers and jesters for three months, but it was the court magicians who captivated me. When one of them changed a rock into a butterfly for the crowd, I got my first glimpse into the possibility of a different life. What if one could transform a man's countenance in just that way, change it from something grotesque to something that was a delight to look upon?

I asked that he teach me the trick; to my disappointment, it was simply sleight of hand, a sleeve pocket into which he slipped the rock, a tiny thread he pulled to awake the butterfly from a sedative doze and send it fluttering into the room.

"But is it not possible," I pressed, "to make the transformation real?"

"Perhaps, but it's not I who can do it."

But living in the palace had many advantages, not the least of which was access to more impressive gossip than one might be privy to in the city. Madrigan was situated on the continent's primary east-west trade route. In addition to the nobles and dignitaries who came to the palace to discuss matters of state, traveling merchants vied to display their wares for palace workers. I kept my ears open during many a meal served to such travelers, as well as during every conversation amongst the entertainers while we waited to appear before the King. That's how I first heard of Laurus, up on Mount Smokestone. Laurus, who could turn a pile of cow dung into gold. Laurus, who could transmute a rat into a steed.

Although Laurus rarely took students, my disfigurement intrigued him, even as it had the King. He said, "If you are not a quick learner, I will not waste my time on you. I will accept nothing less than gold as payment. And it will be years before you're ready to learn what you most want to know."

"I accept those terms."

Laurus kept his hood up through our entire first meeting, so I could discern nothing of his expression. Now I've seen it often enough to know that one eyebrow was surely cocked when he said, "You must bring me twelve gold coins before I will teach you so much as how to turn salt into sugar. Don't come back until you have them."

I saved pennies from my wages at the palace for nearly six months before I returned, but Laurus was true to his word. I'd trained with him ever since, begrudgingly grateful that the King's eccentric tastes kept me in his pay. I quickly learned that no one questioned coins transmuted from rocks, so I never spent a penny I earned at the palace except to pay Laurus. Laurus wouldn't accept the transmuted gold— he alone could sniff out the scent of dirt or copper or whatever it had once been.

In my early years, I earned my keep juggling, balancing grapes on my pointed nose, and telling bawdy stories—the sorts of things that wouldn't be amusing if I stood higher than three-and-a-half feet, with a straight spine, and large, sure hands. My wages increased as I added all I learned from Laurus to my act: changing ladies' handkerchiefs into brocaded robes, transforming ugly black flies into butterflies, turning water to wine (some of the more religious guests got especially worked up about that one).

It was not work I enjoyed, and I didn't need it to pay Laurus now that a baby had become the only price he would accept. But as long as the King desired my services—entertaining three nights a week—I would provide them, seeking a child on my days off. All of us who worked in the palace had heard the whispers, that King Lucas's benign delight in the unusual could be a mere precursor to a darker sort of madness, the sort that had lived in the royal family for generations. We knew stories about palace workers who had displeased his father; how he had beheaded the lead cook because he had prepared fish for a banquet when the King craved chicken; how he had sent a prized advisor to rot in the dungeon based on a rumor that the man wanted to put aside his duties to spend more time with his dying daughter. I was not the only one in the palace who tiptoed around King Lucas, afraid that any displeasure would be enough to awaken his father in him.

Some of those in the King's employ murmured that he needed a woman to soften him and to ward off the madness—for although he had been King nearly ten years, Lucas did not yet have a queen to reign beside him. But those conversations only turned to stories about the previous queen, who had died within five years of marrying Lucas's father, living just long enough to birth the heir. Some said Lucas had no taste for fine women. Others said no one was willing to offer his daughter up to a family with such a reputation—not for all the treasure in Madrigan.

I had the night off the first time I saw her. The sun had barely set, but already I was climbing the stairs to my room, exhausted from another day of dirty looks and protective, angry mothers. Women didn't take it well when you offered to take children off their hands, even if they seemed to want nothing more in the world.

My quarters, though modest, included a bed, warm blankets, and candles, even a chest of drawers with a mirror, should I want to pull up a stool and contemplate my visage—useful for when I needed a reminder of why I mustn't give up my quest for a baby.

I'd spent most of my childhood sleeping in barns or on rugs—the orphanages I lived in from time-to-time couldn't afford to sleep less than two children to a bed, and no one wanted to share a bed with me. I'd come to prefer lying down in the straw with the warmth of a dog curled up beside me, awakening to kittens tumbling over my body or a horse nuzzling my hair. These creatures never flinched when they saw me, or looked away uncomfortably, or fumbled over their words. Now, even though the King supplied me with a proper bed, I still found myself wandering into the stables to feel the horses' soft muzzles or to scratch the dogs behind the ears. That's why I recognized the men who were passing me on the stairs that night; they were the King's stablemen, all hoisting bales of straw on their shoulders.

I caught up with Jeremy, a lad who had always been kind to me. "What is all this?" I asked.

Jeremy glanced around, then lowered his voice. "Another of the King's crazy schemes." The stable boys were in fine shape from mucking out stalls and tossing hay bales, but this work of carrying straw into the tower reddened Jeremy's face, and he panted before he continued: "One of the King's buyers was out in the market today, ran into this man who boasted that his daughter could spin straw into gold. I suspect the buyer only told King Lucas to give him a laugh, but the King took it seriously and demanded she be brought here."

Could it be? Was there another in the city who could do transmutations?

Surely Laurus didn't have other students. I'd been training with him seven years; if he had another student, I would have seen a trace of her by now—passed her in a doorway, seen her footprints on the mountain path, noticed a roll of parchment with her notes left behind in Laurus's study.

"Why the tower?" I asked. "Why not just bring this girl to the stables, or the granary?"

Jeremy shifted the bale upon his shoulder, waiting for another man to pass him on the stairs. Then he whispered, "You know how sensitive the King is about his family's madness. He doesn't want word of this to get out. If the girl can't do these things, he won't be thought crazy for believing it. And if she can, he keeps her to himself."

Jeremy continued upward, and I backed into my room. If what the girl's father claimed was true, perhaps *she* could teach me the final transmutation. And perhaps she'd accept some lesser payment than a child in its first year.

I cracked my door open, hoping I might catch a glimpse of her as she climbed the tower. Eventually, the parade of men and straw bales ceased. Then another small entourage made its way past my door. This one consisted of two guards dressed in the King's red, each of them holding an arm of the woman who walked between them. Woman? Why, she was no more than a girl, wispy and hunched over, as if she wanted to tuck her head between her frail shoulders. The hair that coursed down her back also hid most of her face, but even in the night's gloom I could see that it gleamed golden. Perhaps she *was* advanced enough in her craft to perform transmutations on her own body, and perhaps her hair truly was made of spun gold! If that were true, she may not be a young maiden at all, but a bent old hag. The possibility of such human transmutation made my stomach flutter.

Closing my door, I lit the candles around my dressing table, pulled up a stool, and climbed onto it to see my reflection in the mirror. I caught a glimpse of the excitement on my face—a twinkle in my muddy eyes, an up-turning at the corners of my mouth—before my expression fell. My red, curly hair grew thick over large, protruding ears but left a conspicuous patch of skin uncovered at the top of my forehead. And that forehead was furrowed above prominent brows, no matter how much I tried to relax my countenance. I looked like a stooped man in his eighth decade of life, not a young, hardworking lad just coming into the prime of manhood. Why, what other man of twenty-two had hair already receding from his head, while it sprouted much too enthusiastically from his ears and nostrils?

I reached for the scissors, then snipped at my nose hairs, my ear hairs, even the unruly mess of my eyebrows. I combed through my hair, then reached for my best blue velvet cap. I changed into the breeches and jacket that matched it, as well as a shirt with a lace collar and ruby brooch—all of which I'd purchased with money transmuted from stones. But when I appraised myself in the mirror, I still looked like nothing more than a fool—a fool who got his laughs by the mockery he made of being a gentleman.

I sighed. *Perhaps she's just a transmuted old hag,* I reminded myself. It didn't make me feel better.

Well, I wasn't getting any handsomer. I left my chamber and ascended farther up the tower, to the only room higher than mine, to the room that had stood empty for as long as I'd been employed here.

Outside the wooden door, I straightened myself to the extent that my crooked spine allowed, and knocked.

No response.

I rapped again.

Silence.

"Hello?" I called, before pushing gently on the door. It didn't budge—locked.

"Miss? I work in the palace," I said. "I'm wondering, is there anything you need? Some refreshment, perhaps?"

She had to be in there. Transmutation could cause one thing to change into another, but it could not cause something to disappear. That was another art entirely.

Finally, "No, I'm fine, thank you."

Did I detect the slightest quiver in her voice? My heart softened. Perhaps she really was a girl as young as she appeared.

"I'm going to come in," I said. "I need to talk to you. I won't hurt you."

I closed my eyes and pressed my hands against the door, focusing on the warmth in my palms. Because I performed transmutations for the public, I'd learned to do them by reciting the mantras inside my mind, and I did so now as I changed the door's substance from wood to straw. Might as well give this girl more to work with, eh?

The straw fluttered to the floor. The girl sat crumpled behind a spinning wheel in the corner, her blue eyes wide enough to take up half her face. My heart fell, for her expression revealed all I needed to know. She couldn't transmute.

"What . . . how . . . " And then it wasn't just her voice that was quivering, but her whole body. Her lips began to part, and I knew she was going to scream. I darted across the space between us and clamped my hand over her mouth.

"Don't scream," I whispered. "I won't hurt you. I just want to talk, so don't scream."

Slowly, I removed my hand from her mouth. She stared up at me. "The door." She pointed at the pile of straw in the doorframe. "How did you . . . ?"

"A parlor trick," I muttered. "It's not the same as spinning straw into gold, but it will do in a pinch."

With that, a sob burst forth from her.

"No, I'm sorry . . . whatever your name is." I scrambled to the empty doorway. "I . . . look, just wait a bit, okay?" Kneeling in the straw, I pressed my hands to it. I couldn't drown out the girl's crying, so I muttered the mantras aloud to maintain my focus. When the wooden door was back in place, I dropped the latch down and locked it, then turned to her, brushing straw and wood dust off my hands. "You see? It's as if it never happened."

"But it *did*."

The spinning wheel had a piece of straw awkwardly strung through the spindle. I pulled a straw bale up across from her and sat down. "Look, I'm sorry I frightened you. I just, I thought you could teach me something very important."

She bit her lip. I moved over on the straw bale. "With all these bales of straw, you need not sit on the floor, do you?"

She eyed me warily, but she lifted her skirt from under her and sat beside me on the bale. When she straightened her back, I regretted inviting her up. Now I could see that she was not as young as she'd first appeared; her body displayed a woman's curves. And she dwarfed me when we sat side by side.

"So, what's the problem?" I tried to sound casual.

"I can't do it." She put her hands on her lap. "I'm sorry I panicked, but . . . but I can't do it, and then, that thing with the door, and . . . " She looked at me.

"And I'm tiny and gnarled and ugly, I know."

"Well, I imagine that doesn't matter much, when you can do things like that." She gestured toward the door.

*It matters more than you think.* But what I said was, "So, how did this rumor start that you . . . ?"

"Once I told my father about a dream I used to have about turning straw into gold. Then he said that when I was a child, I would sit at Mother's spinning wheel and claim I was making gold." She shook her head. "Children's nonsense, but Father gets things all mixed up. He hasn't been right in the head since Mother died. He tells these stories, but no one believes him! And now, all this!" She swept her hand toward the straw bales stacked against every wall, the loose straw scattered on the floor.

"Well," I said, "I can."

Her eyes widened. I rolled up my sleeves. She looked at the door, then back at me again.

"What can I give you?" she asked.

I eyed her. Dared I say it? *Well, do you have a baby sister, or a nephew, that you could perhaps do without?*

"Take this," she said, unclasping her necklace and passing it into my hands.

I examined it. It was heart-shaped, crafted of fine gold, with a tiny ruby in the place where the two curves of the heart met. I curled my fingers around it. How could I ask her for a child now? I could tell by the number of times the hem on her dress had been let out that she was poor; she had likely just handed all her wealth over to me.

"Very well," I muttered, slipping the necklace into my pocket. Then, I set to work.

Even Laurus had never set such a task before me. Transmutation is not intended for great quantities; if you're without money and need a meal and a bed, a few stones into coins will do the trick. I glanced at the spinning wheel. A useless prop, but it must be thread if the King was to believe the girl had used it for the transformation. I had never paid much heed to the shimmering gold thread that lined the King's capes, but I would have to picture it perfectly for the transmutation to work.

Again, I mumbled the mantras aloud to maintain concentration, taking care to ignore the girl. I had never been alone with such a beauty. Her golden hair made the thread I proffered from the straw seem mean and low.

I worked through the night, collapsing from exhaustion just as the horizon began slipping from deep blue to gray. My hands burned from the amount of energy I had funneled through them, and my brain felt like mush. I was vaguely aware of movement in the room, but I came to full awareness when I felt cool fingers moving in careful circles on my temples. "You poor thing," murmured the girl. "I'm sorry; I didn't know the work would exhaust you so."

How very different this was from when one of Laurus's assignments exhausted me. When I collapsed on his floor, he merely poked me with the toe of his boot, murmuring, "Perhaps you aren't up to this sort of work after all. Perhaps you wouldn't even survive the final transmutation."

At which point, I would scramble to my feet to prove that I was, in fact, strong enough for whatever he could teach me. Now, the girl had pulled my head upon her lap, her fingers continuing to work on me, and I wanted nothing more than to stay there the whole day through.

Day! I opened my eyes and saw the first traces of sunlight sparkling off the mounds of gold thread. Someone would be here soon to check the girl's work. So I scrambled up, using all my concentration to keep from swaying on my feet. "And now, I must leave you," I said, giving the girl a bow. I was so disoriented by my weariness and the girl's kindness that I was back in my own room before I realized I hadn't gotten her name. And I didn't know if I'd ever see her again.

I drew the necklace out of my pocket, shaking my head. What good was this bauble? I could not transmute it into a child. I hung it upon the edge of my mirror and began pulling off my clothes. I might not ever come across anyone as desperate as that girl had been, and my own timidity or useless conscience had kept me from asking for the only thing in the world I needed.

I slept through the day and awakened when I heard heavy footsteps and men's voices on the stairs. Rubbing my eyes, I poked my head out the door and gaped. Stable hands were going up into the tower with straw bales while the King's guards came down carrying baskets of the gold thread on their shoulders.

"What, again?" I asked.

One of the stable hands nodded toward the baskets of gold thread. "I don't know how, but she did it," he gasped. "Now the King wants her to do it again."

My stomach rumbled, and my legs still trembled with weariness. I ducked back inside, quickly dressed, washed my face, and combed through my tangle of hair. Then I went down to the kitchen.

Like most of the palace workers, I ate in the kitchen, out of sight. Even on nights when I was performing, it turned the stomachs of some guests to have me dine near them. I didn't mind. The kitchen was the best place to absorb gossip. When I asked the lead cook, Gertrude, about the girl, she was eager to talk.

"The King has his tailor and his goldsmith assessing each skein of thread," she said, "determining what its worth might be. It's the real thing, but I don't expect I'll see any of it, nor you. It will just go to line the King's bed curtains, or be sold to fill his coffers."

"It's trickery," said Ilsa, a young, brown-haired cook. She flopped a blob of dough on the table and began rolling it out. "I know Emily's family; they live twelve strong in one small cottage. Her mother died three years ago birthing the last baby; her dad has been daft ever since. If she can turn straw into gold, why didn't she buy her family a home with more room? Or at least patch a few of their tattered dresses!"

Emily. That was her name.

"They ought to have someone watch her tonight," said Ilsa, "to see what's really happening in that tower."

Gertrude shook her head. "She claims the feat is impossible to perform without complete privacy." Shrugging, she added, "If it's a lie, she might be able to pull it off for one night—but three nights in a row? If she can't do it, she'll be found out. And if she can, King Lucas collects easy money!"

Three nights. The news both dismayed and delighted me. I didn't relish the thought of two more nights of work like the last one. But this also meant I hadn't lost my chance. I brought my bowl to the stew pot for a large second helping.

That night, I knocked on the door of Emily's tower room once more. This time, she called, "Who's there?"

"Your humble assistant," I replied. I heard the latch lift, and she opened the door.

When she saw me, her eyes lit, and my heart jerked. Never had I seen joy on a woman's face when she looked at me.

She grasped my hands, pulling me inside and locking the door behind us. "Oh, thank heavens," she breathed. I assessed the room, straw bales lining every wall.

"There's more here than last night," I observed.

She worked at a ruby ring on her finger, then held it toward me. "For payment," she said.

I looked up at her. Her jaw was set, her face resolute and still, but her fingers trembled while she waited for me to accept the ring. I sighed, took it, and set to my second night's work.

Emily remained silent until my work was done, at which point I collapsed at her feet. She bent and brushed my hair away from my face. "Dawn is not yet here," she murmured. "Take some time to rest, my tiny hero."

My exhaustion was not enough to stop the corners of my mouth from curving in a smile.

"What is your name?" she asked.

My eyes popped open. Laurus had told me that Rumpelstiltskin might be a fine name for someone bent and ugly, but that it was no name for the man I would become. I spent much time imagining a name for that new man—Paul, perhaps, or Tom. I didn't want to offer Emily this name that was as ugly as the rest of me; I wanted to wait until I could be as much a pleasure for her eyes as she was for mine.

"It's an ugly, twisted name," I muttered, "for an ugly, twisted body. I prefer 'tiny hero.'"

"What does a twisted body matter, to someone with power like yours? Power is more useful than beauty."

*Easy for someone beautiful to say.* Suddenly my heart seemed to shrink. Why was I letting this girl caress me as if we might be lovers and placate me with her little trinkets? Ilsa knew her family; there wasn't a child in it younger than three. I was wasting my time. Perhaps if I were Paul or Tom I could lie with my head in her lap forever. But I was Rumpelstiltskin, and anyone who saw this spectacle would think it pathetic.

I rose. "I must go before they come to check your work." My tone was clipped, and I thought I saw a flicker of hurt in her eyes. Probably she was used to having the world adore her, probably she knew nothing about being left abruptly. It was foolish for me to do this, to work harder than I'd ever worked before, for useless jewelry. Yet, even as I closed the door behind me, I knew I would return for one more night.

*I, Laurus of Mount Smokestone, do hereby promise to share the secrets of human transmutation with my pupil, Rumpelstiltskin of Madrigan, in exchange for a child in its first year of life. Should I refuse to provide the agreed-upon instruction, I shall eat but always be hungry, sleep but always be weary, shiver with cold even when seated before a blazing fire, reminded by my body at every moment that I have violated this magically binding agreement.*

I had read the agreement so many times that I had memorized it. Still, running my fingers over Laurus's signature strengthened my resolve. The agreement was ensorcelled, and bringing Laurus a child would activate it. If he did not provide me with the promised exchange, the magic in the document would be released, meting out Laurus's punishment.

Rolling the agreement up, I slipped it back into the drawer. It was Emily's last night in the palace—and my last chance.

I felt bone tired before I even began to work.

"I was afraid you wouldn't return," Emily said. She was rubbing her thumb against the finger that once wore her ring. I considered giving the damn thing back.

"It's the last night," she rushed on. "After tonight, he'll let me go."

I nodded wearily.

"I have nothing more to offer." She spread her empty hands. "But please, if I can't do it tonight, my father will be killed for his lies, and perhaps me as well, and no one is as good at managing the household as I am. Peter does all right with the money and Josie is good with the little ones, but I'm best with keeping it all running, and in setting Father right when his mind goes too far astray. . . ."

"There is one thing I want," I said, my voice perfectly steady. I was not going to let my heart leap and quiver tonight; tonight, it was time I got something more lasting than her sweet, soft touches.

"I told you, I have—"

"I want your firstborn child."

Her mouth remained open from her unfinished protest. She closed it, dropping her eyes. "I have no children."

"But you will, someday. Doesn't every woman?"

"I have no husband."

"You'll have that, too. You're pretty enough. Besides, last I checked, husbands weren't necessary to get babies."

She nodded, but she still didn't look at me. "All right," she said. "My mother, my sweetheart, and my child, these are the offerings I make to spare my father's life and return home."

I had no interest in her dead mother, her nameless sweetheart. It would do me no good to follow her pretty little mysteries wherever they may lead; the bargain was made.

I set to work, closer to my goal than ever before. And thank goodness, because I had never felt uglier.

At the end of the night, I didn't allow myself to succumb to fatigue. Instead, I stood on quivering legs, swayed, and reached for the door latch to steady myself. "It is done," I said. "I look forward to seeing you when you are big with child."

I turned away, but I felt her hand on my shoulder. "How will I find you?" she asked. "I don't even know your name."

"Haven't you noticed? I don't exactly look like the other men you'd pass on the street. Just ask anyone about the crumpled magician who works in the palace."

She came around me, turned me toward her. She placed her soft hands on either side of my face.

If she didn't come for me when she was with child, or if she were barren and never bore a child, this might be the last time those blue eyes would fix upon me. What kind of fool was I, to think she would come to me when she carried her most precious creation within her? I knew nothing about this girl except that she had no qualms about working a tiny man to exhaustion three nights in a row. "If you don't come to me, then I will call upon you," I said, "once with each change of the moon, to see how close I come to collecting my final payment. That's when we'll meet again."

I began to pull away, but she held me, whispered, "Thank you," and then she was bending forward, and her lips were covering mine. My eyes remained wide open despite a temptation to let my whole body dissolve into a puddle at her feet.

What nonsense! I put my hands on her face, pushed her away. "Rumpelstiltskin," I muttered, wiping a hand across my mouth. "That is my name, if you must know."

And I turned away once more, slamming the door behind me.

For all my exhaustion, sleep did not come easily. My body hummed with the memory of Emily's recent closeness. I wished I had not so hastily wiped away her kiss, for I wanted to bring the feeling of her lips' soft moistness back again. But I had not wanted her to see that her kiss had affected me so.

The effect was persistent, nonetheless. I closed my eyes, wishing it wasn't she I saw behind them.

I awoke to a loud pounding on the door. "Rumpelstiltskin! The entertaining has already begun; your performance is in five minutes."

I scrambled out of bed. I'd forgotten that it was a Thursday. The King's first guests always started trickling into town on Thursdays. They were weary from their journey and desired only half an hour of mindless amusement before they drifted to their rooms. I donned my costume—a yellow and red jester's uniform with a floppy, tasseled, bell-laden hat—and grabbed my bag of props. I finally wiped the sleep from my eyes just before I tumbled into the center of the Great Hall amidst the laughter of the guests.

I always began my routine facing the King. Emily sat in a small, ornate chair at his side, wearing a fine silk dress of rich red and gold. Although her eyes sparked when she saw me, that didn't hide the weariness in them. She looked more tired than I felt.

I had done my act so often that I didn't need to think about it, so I don't believe Emily's presence had any noticeable effect on my performance. But as flowers turned into butterflies that landed on the hands of ladies in the court, as appreciative murmurs and coins drifted my way, I couldn't stop wondering, *Why is she still here?*

The audience applauded and laughed as I gave my final bows. The King rose from his throne, clapping his large hands slowly and emphatically, the sound hanging in the air even after the rest of the crowd quieted. "Thank you, Rumpelstiltskin, for that delightful display." He paused, looked out at the guests gathered. "It is my desire that you should all feel as enchanted tonight as I do, although I daresay your amusement at my dwarf's performance pales against the joy I carry in my heart. For you see, I have chosen a bride."

A murmur rippled through the crowd. My legs felt rooted to the middle of the floor, the pit of my stomach a heavy ball of ice. The King reached for Emily's hand, and she rose beside him, a wan smile trembling on her lips. He said, "It is true that my dear Emily is not born of noble blood—but one look at her, and I'm sure you'll agree she has beauty and grace to rival that of any princess. Indeed, I cannot imagine any bride making me feel richer."

Emily locked her eyes on mine.

*Good Lord, would this ever end?*

After the King's announcement, the musicians began playing, and I realized there would be dancing tonight. I felt a pang of sympathy for the guests who were obligated to celebrate the King's betrothal when they probably wanted to go to bed as much as I did. As an unofficial part of my routine, I always danced the first couple numbers, swirling amongst the women's billowing dresses and the men's quick feet. When I grew weary and stepped off to the side, Emily found me.

"I've come to tell you how delightful your performance was!" She raised her voice to be heard over the music, or perhaps so the other guests would know the nature of our conversation. Then she leaned in closer and whispered, "You must help me again, dear Rumpelstiltskin. Where can I find you?"

I frowned, not at all sure I wanted to continue this arrangement. I already had what I wanted from her. But she was a simple ceremony away from becoming Queen. I would be wise to remain on her good side.

"The tower," I told her, "the one where you performed your miracles. Don't take the steps all the way to the top; my room is on the second-highest floor."

I returned to my room nearly two hours after midnight. Lord, but my head throbbed. I sank onto the bed, rubbing my temples. Emily was marrying the King. Her firstborn child would have royal blood, a much higher payment than even Laurus demanded. Securing this child would take careful planning indeed; if the King suspected me, my final performance would include my head rolling off the chopping block.

But if it worked! If it worked, perhaps I could make my transformation before the King discovered what had happened to the child. He could turn the kingdom upside down in search of Rumpelstiltskin, never recognizing him in the handsome face that would soon be mine.

A light knock sounded on my door. My breath caught. *Already?* I glanced down at myself, feeling foolish to still be in my jester's uniform. Heaving a sigh, I opened the door.

Emily stood there, no longer in her finery, but in a white gown that fell all the way to her feet, which were encased in white stockings. I shut the door behind her and said, "How is it that you already have free rein of the palace?"

A blush colored her cheeks. "These last three mornings, I've slipped a bit of the gold thread into my pockets before the King's men arrived to check my work. I've used it to buy my guard's silence. He escorted me all the way to the foot of this tower."

I shook my head, remembering the wide-eyed, frantic look upon her face the first time she saw me. I'd taken her then for just another silly—albeit, beautiful—girl. But I was beginning to suspect something else, a carefully hidden cunning. My belly rolled uneasily.

"This is my plan," she continued. "I've told the King I cannot perform my magic for an audience; it requires intense concentration and privacy to work. I've also told him that the amount of work he's put me through these last three nights has drained me, and that I need some time to rest before being asked to do it again." She laughed nervously. "Also, there's no spinning wheel in my room."

I waved my hand dismissively. "Keep up that spinning wheel ruse as long as you'd like. But you saw the wheel has nothing to do with transmutation."

"I still can't believe what I *did* see. But I know that it exhausted you. I couldn't ask you to do this throughout our marriage."

*OUR marriage?* She and the King. The King. Not she and I.

"So I thought, perhaps, you could teach me to do what you do."

My eyes widened. This was not the request I expected. "I don't know, Emily. I've never taught it before. I'm a transmuter, a cheap performer, not a teacher."

"Then it *can* be taught!" She clasped her hands together. "I was afraid that it was something you were born with, something you couldn't transfer to me, no matter how hard I tried."

"It can be taught," I acknowledged begrudgingly. I looked up at her. "When is the wedding?"

"In three months, on the tenth anniversary of the King's coronation."

I sighed.

"I'll pay you," she said in a rush.

"I don't want any more jewelry, I have no use for gold coins, and one child is sufficient."

"I have none of those things. But what I do have, I offer for as long as you desire." Her fingers moved to the laces at the top of her nightgown, and she began to untie them.

Should I have refused her? Should I have forgotten all those tiny touches and kisses from our three nights together, the way she had continued to sing in my body even after I closed the door between us? It was never she who repelled me, but my certainty that these desires would never reach fruition. And it was a lifetime of nights spent without such caresses that drove me toward the final transmutation. At least now when I made my transformation, I wouldn't enter my new life totally ignorant in the ways of love.

She had not slept during the day as I had, and so she was too tired to begin learning that night. But she had enough energy to offer her first payment.

Every night, we spent three hours together after the rest of the palace had gone to sleep. The first two hours, I taught her to calm her mind, to feel and direct the magic we all carry in our bodies, to memorize the incantations. I explained to her that neither the straw nor the gold thread were significant to transmutation. "I simply used what you'd been given to create something that matched the expectation. But once you learn to transform one substance to another, you can create thread from dust or rocks or a pile of dung. Or you can create coins or buttons or parchment, for all I care. The principle is the same, regardless."

But despite Emily's dedication, I could not coax a single transmutation from her hands even after weeks of teaching. One night, in frustration, I said, "Perhaps if you *feel* what happens when I transmute . . ."

I rummaged around my room until I found a length of cord. I took one of her hands and placed it atop my own, both hands palms down. Then I bound our wrists together and reached for the empty glass upon my desk. As I attempted to transmute it into a block of gold, Emily gasped and tried to jerk away at the feel of the power passing through my fingers. I dropped the glass before the transmutation took hold, and it shattered upon the floor.

"You see?" I said. "This is painful, Emily. If you want to learn this, you mustn't fear it. Respect it, yes, but don't fear it. Magic is like a wild horse; if it senses your fear, it will trample you."

Emily was trembling, her eyes fixed upon our knotted hands. My anger dissolved at the sight of her slender, white hand cupped over my own gnarled, hairy one. It was then that I realized I'd mirrored the simple hand-fasting wedding ceremonies the peasants employed. With my other hand, I transmuted the cord into rose petals that softly fell away from our wrists, setting her free.

The men in the taverns said there were two things that could make a man spill his secrets: too much wine, and the face of a pretty girl.

I didn't want to desire more from Emily than what she offered, which was already more than I'd ever expected before the final transmutation. Yet when our romp was through each night, I found myself wishing she would linger. I curled my hand around her back, watched the candlelight flicker on her mussed golden hair, watched the shadows that dipped into the triangle indentation at the base of her neck. Tonight, her eyes were open, but they were not on me; I followed the direction of her gaze until my eyes landed upon my mirror, the heart-shaped necklace hooked over its edge. It winked in the candlelight.

"What will you do with it?" Emily asked. "Will it fetch a good price? Will you give it to some future sweetheart?"

I snorted. But then, I'd almost forgotten I was no longer doomed to this life forever. When Emily married the King, she would have a child, and I would have my final teachings. And I certainly *did* intend to have sweethearts when I had a body that did not have to squeeze its caresses out of pity.

"Is that where you got it?" I asked, and my hand slid off her back. I remembered now, her mention of a sweetheart, and I wanted to scurry for the blankets at the foot of the bed, hide myself from her. Had she lain with him? Perhaps she even imagined him when she was with me.

As she shook her head, her hair brushed against my shoulder. I looked at her then, saw that moisture glistened at the corners of her eyes just as the necklace glistened. Lord, I had upset her.

"My mother," she said. "It was my mother's. I told you how my father wasn't the same after she died. He couldn't focus at work, he wasn't keeping up with the accounts. Every week, I went to the coffer to buy the things our household needed, and every week, I noticed that the coins were never refilled. Asking Father about it was useless. All he ever said was, 'Oh, things are slow right now, but I expect they'll pick up soon.' Meanwhile, angry customers were showing up at our house because they'd dropped off their corn or their wheat at the mill and had never gotten anything back. I didn't want to do it, but I took out Mother's things, seeing what she had left that we could sell. We were already reusing all of her clothes, but her jewelry . . . it wasn't practical to keep it around when we needed to eat. I brought it to the market, but I held on to the necklace longest, because she was never without it. Father gave it to her to seal his promise when she accepted his marriage proposal, so to sell it made me feel as though I were betraying them both.

"At last, a young man came who wanted to purchase it. He had—no, never mind. It doesn't matter what he looked like."

I felt a constriction at my neck, as if, naked though I was, I'd buttoned a collar too tight. "Tell me," I said. "It's your story. Tell it as you like."

At least I could take it as an education. Learn by the tone of her voice what it was that women found appealing in a man, and what they did not.

"He had eyes that were the color of chocolate," she said, and now her voice caught. "Have you ever seen chocolate?"

"I have. I live in the palace."

"Of course." She blushed; and as she did, I wondered where she, a peasant, had ever seen the expensive imported drink. "He was tall, and when he took the necklace from my hands, I could see he was strong. I had seen him wandering the marketplace before, standing at this stall or another, always carefully considering. Always he was dressed the same, in straight black breeches and an airy white shirt, clothes that didn't speak of one profession or another. Although I'd seen him around, I never knew where he'd come from. Most families have been in Madrigan for generations; but his family was unknown to me. Somehow, I didn't want Mother's necklace to go to someone I knew nothing about. So I asked an unreasonable price—a price that could feed our family for three months at least. He reached into his purse, and offered it."

My jaw was tight. *I could have done the same,* I thought.

"I asked him if it was for his sweetheart," she continued. "And he said, 'Perhaps, if I am so lucky. It is a gift for the most beautiful girl in the city.'

"And as I looked away to deposit the sum he'd given me, I felt something brush against my neck. He was lifting my hair, fastening the necklace. At first I thought it was some sort of joke; I tried to take it off, for precious as it was, I didn't dare part with the money it had fetched. He said, 'No, no. Keep the money and the necklace both—but for the price, allow me only to see it upon you every day.'"

"So he was your sweetheart." I tried to keep a grumble from my voice.

"After that day, yes."

"And the ring?"

"That was a sign of his promise to me when I agreed to marry him."

I pushed out of bed, not wanting to think of her with this straight-backed man whose eyes were delicious to her. But then—perhaps he was not what he seemed? She hadn't married him, after all, and the sum he'd paid her had run out, or she wouldn't have arrived at the palace as desperate as she was all those weeks ago. He had been a vagabond, no doubt, one of those men who breezes through town and throws money around and breaks the heart of the prettiest girl he finds.

When I turned back to her, her eyes were so wide they swallowed the room's candlelight. She'd drawn the sheet up to cover her body, but it did nothing to conceal her beauty. *She was watching me.* She did not avert her eyes from *my* nakedness. I was so used to stares or eyes that avoided me altogether, but not this. Not this just *looking.*

I had to crawl onto a stool to retrieve the necklace from the mirror. But I brought it back to her, knelt over her in the bed, lifted her neck from the pillow. My hands were steady as I returned it to her neck. I tried not to think of her sweetheart doing the same.

She touched it. "No, please," she whispered. "You must keep teaching me."

"This is not a return on our agreement," I said. "It's only that it would look quite ridiculous on my stump of a neck."

Her smile wavered. I wondered if she was thinking what I was: the ring from her sweetheart would never fit past my first knuckle. But that, I did not return.

For the remainder of the week, I was snappish with her. As much as I told myself I did not want to know about her beautiful man, curiosity gnawed at me. We were halfway to the wedding date, and Emily had begun telling her guard that she was going to the tower to use the spinning wheel when she left for her sessions with me. Now, the stable hands always left a bale or two of straw up there for her. Still, she had not yet transmuted a single item. Instead, I sent her back to her room with skeins of silken gold that *I* had transmuted. She, in turn, scattered them casually about her room.

I opened my drawer of odds and ends, rummaging until I found the ruby ring. I placed it in my palm and held it out to her. I would remove this last reminder of her suitor. "It's real gold, yes?"

She nodded.

"That might make it easier; perhaps we've started too large. Perhaps we should start with a single material, and transform it into something different but of the same substance. We have here a gold ring. Let us transmute it into a gold coin."

This was not how Laurus had started with me, but it was worth a try.

But in the end, it was once again I who turned the ring into a coin. It glinted faintly red in the candlelight, as if it remembered the ruby stone it once held.

"Can you change it back?" she asked.

"Of course. But it's better I don't. You shouldn't have this reminder of your former suitor lingering about six weeks before you marry the King. It could drive him mad with jealousy if he found out—and that could be very dangerous indeed."

She nodded, solemnly studying the coin in her palm. She slipped it into her pocket.

"Best *you're* free of the reminder, too," I muttered. "What good is it to pine for a man who can't even make good his promise of marriage?"

She stood up straighter. "You don't know anything about him."

*I know that he was tall, dark, handsome—isn't that enough? I know that you loved him because you spoke as much about him as you possibly could, even though you were supposed to be telling a story about your dear dead mother.* But instead, I said, "Fine. Tell me."

She did. She told me that he was a traveling merchant, buying goods in one city and then traversing the land, bringing them to villages where the people had never seen such things, and fetching higher prices for them. She told me how he would be away for long stretches at a time, traveling with one caravan or another, and how, when he came back, he always brought her silk or candies or carved stones. Sometimes he was gone for weeks, months. And then, he'd taken a journey from which he'd never returned.

"He was distracted by another beautiful maiden, no doubt." I bent to remove my boots. Let the lesson be concluded for tonight—I wanted my reminder that, sweetheart or no, King or no, for these few precious months, Emily was mine. "You are not the only one in the world, you know."

She bit her lip, and I hated myself. What I said may have been true enough—but whenever she was in my room, I had difficulty believing it. A troubling thought had been keeping me up nights: what if, even after the final transmutation, I could not find a woman I wanted as much as I wanted Emily? These thoughts aroused in me a certain hatred for her, which spilled out in moments like this.

"It could have been anything," she said. "I worried about him every time he left. Robbers attack traveling merchants all the time. Sometimes he returned with cuts upon his forehead, with bruises on his body. He wouldn't have just left me. Something happened to him. And now, if he ever returns, he'll find that I've betrayed him by marrying another."

"Accepting a king's proposal is hardly a betrayal." I was now working my shirt buttons, growing impatient with this conversation. "Do you think I enjoy making an ass of myself in front of his court three nights a week? Now that my training has come to a halt, I don't even need his coins. But you don't say no when the King wants something. Ugly though it is, I prefer to keep my head attached to my body, thank you very much. And I would rather rest in this bedroom than a dungeon cell. So would you, I suspect."

"Training?" repeated Emily, and I froze. For the first time, I'd let slip a hint of my life outside the palace, outside weekends entertaining the King and evenings teaching Emily.

"It is nothing." I waved my hand dismissively. "It is only that I wish to learn something bigger than turning rocks to gold."

"I would be happy to learn only that." Emily slumped onto my bed—which was where I wanted her, anyway. I shrugged my shirt off my shoulders and approached her.

"You will," I said, although I also had trouble believing it. I crawled up onto the bed beside her, kissed her neck. "We have time."

But for the first time ever, she pulled away from me. What? Had it taken her this long to notice I was repulsive?

"I'm not even sure I believe this is possible anymore," she said. "I'm just a commoner, a miller's daughter. How many times can I watch you turn anything you touch into gold, or feel your fingers while you do it, or do everything you tell me to do, only to find myself holding the same old stone or button or piece of string in the end?"

"It's not easy. Remember, I've been doing this for many, many years."

"I just don't think I *have it*, Rumpel. Whatever it is that allows you to do this. How long did it take you to do your first transmutation?"

That arrested me. I remembered those early days with Laurus, the way I knew, the first time I transformed a palm full of salt into a palm full of sugar, that surely this gift could be more than kitchen magic if I could only harness it. That this gift could be the key to achieving what I'd always believed to be impossible. "Three days," I mumbled. "I made my first transmutation three days after I began my instruction."

"You see?" She stood now, agitated. "If this is something so easily taught, why isn't the whole world clamoring to learn it? I've never met anyone like you before, nor have I met anyone with this particular gift. What about your teacher? Was he like you?"

I narrowed my eyes. "What do you mean, like me?"

She gestured vaguely. "You know . . ."

"Ugly?" I spat. "Twisted? Puny? No, he's none of those things." And yet, I thought about the way Laurus preferred to keep his hood up, how, when I had seen his face, I'd noticed that his skin was paler than bone; indeed, it stretched so tightly over his skull that it might as well have *been* bone. But he was old, and he'd told me often how a lifetime of channeling such power could take its toll on a body.

"I just don't think I have it in me. This power."

*But you have the power to make a king want to take you as his wife; you have the power to make me forget what other women look like, so that all I can see is the length of your golden hair, the curve of your back when you lie on your stomach. This is powerful magic indeed, and surely, teaching you to bend it into a form that serves you differently is just another transmutation.*

The next time Emily came to me, she said, "I have told you all about my life. Now you must tell me something about you."

I crossed my arms. "The sharing of secrets was not part of our agreement."

"Why do you want my child?"

"I want *a* child. Yours just happens to be the most convenient."

She stamped her foot. "Damn it, Rumpel. Just tell me."

"It's none of your business."

"It's *my* child!"

When I said nothing, she asked softly, "Is it because of the way you are? Are you unable to sire children of your own?"

Her words sent a pang through me. Before this, I'd never given much thought to children; the possibility of a family had always been one of those vague notions that waited for me, perhaps, on the other side of the final transmutation. But all I said to Emily was, "I do not know, and I do not care."

She twisted her gown in her hands. "Can you assure me that no harm will come to it?"

"Harm comes to every child. It's unavoidable."

When she winced, I added, "I would not take it as my purpose to hurt a child, Emily. I am not a monster, regardless of how I look." I reached for her hand. "Come. Let's get started."

She shook her head. "I don't think this is doing either of us any good. We've already taken enough from each other."

Before I could protest, she had turned away, closing the door behind her.

For the rest of the week, Emily stayed away. I tried to tell myself it was of no concern to me. What did I care, if she never learned to transmute?

Without Emily's visits, I could at least catch up on my sleep. That is, if I didn't spend so much time staring at the ceiling, or waking in the middle of the night aching for want of her. But she had never been mine, not really. It was just as well that I got used to it. Soon she'd be in the King's bed. And then she'd have her first child.

After Laurus taught me the final transmutation, I would have other women to take the edge off these long nights. At the end of that first week without Emily, I remembered I *did* have her promise. Perhaps if I brought Laurus proof, it would be enough. With a beautiful body and all the transmuted gold I needed, I could make a new life, far from all this.

The next day, I bent over my desk and wrote out an agreement for Emily. Satisfied, I dressed in my blue velvet suit, rolled the parchment up, and marched to the guard who stood outside Emily's chambers. "Is

Mistress Emily in?" I inquired. "The King bids me to get her approval of the act I will perform at the wedding."

"She's in," grunted the guard. He opened the door.

The ease with which I could visit Emily surprised me. Perhaps it was because she was not yet royalty, or because my excuse seemed plausible—or perhaps a man as muscled and able as the guard perceived no threat to her virtue from a visitor like me.

I entered into a sitting room, blinking against the sunlight spilling through the large windows. Emily sat at a small table, bent over a ream of parchment, her brow creased. It was the first time I'd seen her in full daylight, and for a moment I stood transfixed by the gold of her hair, the white spot of sunlight flashing on the curve of her wrist as she wrote. Perhaps it was only that I'd been starved of her for a week that made her so lovely to me now.

I cleared my throat. She glanced at me, then tapped her quill against the jar of ink upon the table. "Hello, Rumpelstiltskin." Her voice was cool.

"Hello, Emily. I'm sorry to disturb you. This will only take a moment."

I slid a chair up next to hers. I glanced at the parchment already on the table. It was a list of menu options with Emily's notations. I spread the contract out before her and pulled the quill out of the ink. "If you could sign this, please."

At first, Emily only scanned the writing; then her gaze slowed. Her hand, poised to write, slowly dropped to the table.

*I, Emily of Madrigan, do hereby promise my firstborn child to Rumpelstiltskin of Madrigan, for past services already rendered in full. Should I fail to uphold this agreement, I understand that, as the past services cannot be forfeit, certain claims made by me will be brought to light, regardless of the consequences.*

"You would tell the King I didn't do it," she murmured.

I hardened myself against the hurt in her voice. She had known the terms. "It's only fair."

"He might put me to death. Or harm my father."

I clasped my hands behind my back, resisting the urge to reach out and touch her face, take her hand. I could not comfort her; she might exploit such softness.

"I doubt you would have made such an agreement, were the stakes not as high as they are."

She looked at me then, and I fought not to squirm under her gaze. It was steady, almost expressionless, even on the verge of being cold. "It is as you say," she murmured, and signed her name.

Once more, I returned to Laurus's keep. When he opened the door, his face was shrouded in its hood, but I could feel his gaze traveling over me.

"I see you come empty-handed," he said flatly. He did not move aside for me to enter.

"Not quite." I procured the contract from a pocket and passed it up to him.

"This is not a child." Although disdain edged his voice, he took the rolled parchment.

"It's almost as good as one," I said. I glanced around him into the hall. The wind on the mountain was cold, and I hoped he might invite me inside.

Instead, he opened the scroll right there, reading it quickly.

"Very good." He handed it back to me. "You may return when she fulfills this promise."

"Sir, I thought perhaps . . . well, perhaps now that you have the contract in hand, we could begin with the final transmutation." I held the contract limply between us, not wanting to tuck it away lest it signal the end of the discussion.

"A contract is not a child, Rumpelstiltskin."

"No, but she is to be married in less than five weeks. I expect everything will happen quite quickly after that." I tried to push down the sick feeling rising up within me at the thought of her wedding, the thought of her and the King creating the child that would fulfill this contract.

"The contract isn't magically binding." He gestured half-heartedly at it.

"No—but I happen to know she's told a lie that, if exposed, could cost her life—and the lives of others she loves. The stakes are too high for her to refuse."

Laurus sighed as if I were a particularly dense child. "The stakes are never too high when it comes to a woman's child. Many a woman has given her life over for the sake of her babe's, with many more who would do the same if the opportunity arose. Until you arrive at my door with the squalling brat in your arms, it means nothing to me."

The door closed in my face. Before I turned away, I pulled my cloak tight against the chill that had begun to rattle my bones.

When Emily stayed away for another week, I began to sleep more deeply. I really was better off without her. But when a knock on my door roused me, my heart leaped with hope, annoyance following behind it. I scowled as I opened the door.

Emily held out her hand to me.

I stared at it, still bleary-eyed, then took it in my own. I caught the glint of a red jewel upon her finger. "What is this? You woke me just to show me some bauble the King gave you?"

But then I blinked. I knew this ring. I ushered Emily inside, closed the door behind her. "What is the meaning of this?" I hissed.

"I did it. I changed it back."

"You *transmuted* it?"

She nodded.

I wouldn't dwell on the fact that she'd used her newfound gift to return her sweetheart's token to her finger. What mattered was that she had done it! After weeks of us taking our frustration out on one another, all those sleepless nights had paid off. I climbed onto my stool and said, "Well then, let's see it. Change this." I tossed her a copper coin from a pile of the night's tips.

Color rose to her cheeks. "I feel embarrassed to do it with you watching."

"I've seen more than that from you, girl. Come on."

She closed her eyes and began moving her lips in the mantras I had taught her. Her face was so much softer in the light from my one flickering candle than in the brighter light of the King's lamps when she sat beside him at parties. This was the Emily I loved to see best, the one who was far from his side, the one who shared her stories and her secrets and even her body with me.

I shook my head, forcing my gaze to leave her face. It settled upon her hands in time to see them emit a small glow, as though she had caught a firefly. When she opened them again, the copper coin had become a gold one. I took the coin; it was still hot from the magic, but its weight was more substantial than the copper I'd given her. A true transmutation!

"How did you do it?" I was too intrigued to care that she'd managed to do this in her weeks away from me.

"I hardly know," she admitted. "After I left here, transmutation was the last thing I wanted to think about. I was so tired of it all. But as the days passed, thoughts of it started pressing into my mind. At first I could push them away. But eventually, they became an obsession. I could think of nothing but attempting transmutation again. I told myself that if I failed, I could more easily put it from my mind. But somehow I knew I would not fail."

"And you did not." But her success puzzled me. Did mastering transmutation require periods of latency? After all, I only saw Laurus once a week, and the journey to his keep gave me a break even from the lesser transmutations I performed during my acts. Perhaps I'd never realized that the time between instruction was crucial to building the power. Perhaps our schedule of constant training had beaten Emily's power back into some corner, and only the period of rest had coaxed it out.

"You see?" I said. "You had the power in you all along."

"I guess this is it, then." Emily averted her gaze. "I hope you'll let me call on you, if I need help again."

"Of course." My voice was steady, but inside I trembled. Before this moment, I hadn't allowed myself to realize what Emily's mastery of transmutation meant for us. The signed contract I so prized held little weight now. How could I expose her lie when she *could* transmute?

"I believe this brings our arrangement to an end." She shook my hand. "I will not trouble you further, Rumpelstiltskin."

What could I say to that? I could bark out, *Good riddance!*, or I could take her hand and say, *But perhaps now we could be friends*, but both responses stuck in my throat. What I finally managed, as I opened the door for her, was, "Congratulations."

After that, I no longer saw Emily at the King's side. The first couple nights she was absent, the King said nothing of it. The guests said plenty, whispering about whether the two had quarreled. On the third night the King sat alone, he said, "No doubt you wonder why you do not see my future bride beside me. In truth, she is beset with all the little details of weddings that so consume women. She must oversee all the final preparations, which have wearied her."

I narrowed my eyes at the King as I hoisted myself onto a stool to reach a mug of ale. Were we to believe the wedding preparations were enough to exhaust her, even as he continued to attend these parties despite the business of running a kingdom?

Gossip in the kitchen was no more illuminating; for once, the servants took King Lucas at his word. But then, none of them knew Emily as I did; they did not know she could study and make love with me through half the night and still spend all day at the King's side.

I did not see Emily again until the wedding. She traversed the Great Hall's long aisle adorned in a dress of gold, her face so pale it almost faded away behind her veil. Gone was the rush of color I'd seen when something I'd said embarrassed her, gone was the spark in her eyes that had turned to a full flame when she demanded I tell her my intentions for the child. Although her hair retained a gold luster that put her gown to shame, its shine also made her skin appear more sallow. The veil must have trapped her assent to the marriage vows, for all I heard from my place in the back of the Great Hall were the booming voices of the bishop and the King.

Was the King working her too hard, now that she did her own transmutations? My hands curled into fists. I should have continued helping her. Her gift was too new, too fragile. I should have been supplementing it with my own, these last few weeks.

Although she hardly appeared as beautiful as I knew her to be, still I could not take my eyes off her.

At the wedding banquet, the King rose, pulling Emily up with him. He announced, "Each of you will find golden thread encircling the stem of your goblet.

This is Emily's gift to you, her people, on the day she becomes Queen."

I saw Emily's first smile of the day then, as a blush crept up her cheeks. Those gathered may have taken it for modesty; but I wondered if she might be thinking, as I was, about what we had done those nights she was learning to transmute. Or perhaps it was only that I could not bear the thought of anything about this day bringing her happiness. I scowled, casting my eyes about in hopes of finding an empty place setting.

I had no goblet and had taken my portion of the feast in the kitchen already. Still, my fingers itched to touch the thread. I would know, if I held it in my hand, how newly it had been transmuted. Laurus claimed he could smell magic; I could not. But I had noticed that changed objects retained a slight warmth for hours, sometimes days, afterward. If this golden thread had been snipped from the skeins I'd transmuted three months ago, the warmth would be gone.

As the long night of drinking and laughing and dancing continued, some guests became careless and left their golden thread upon the table unattended. I unwound a piece from a goblet, my eyes darting about lest the owner come back for it. Feeling the expected warmth as I pinched the thread between my fingers, I glanced to where Emily sat at the head table. What had this been two days ago? A button, ribbon, stone, feather?

How I wanted to press it into Emily's hand and say, "What was it? Do you remember? Is this what has made you so weary?"

*He will exhaust her*, I thought. *That greedy bastard.*

Before tonight, I had hardly spared any feelings for the King. Now, I hated him.

Seeing Emily at the King's side on the nights I entertained did little to reassure me. Even the bright velvet gowns she now wore could not fool me into believing the color had come back to her skin. She smiled little and spoke less. Although I often strove to catch her eye as I turned a trick or made my bow, she did not return the favor.

And so her mysterious despondency, whatever its cause, became my own. Sleep came harder to me than it ever had those nights I stayed awake teaching her and, later, touching her. After a month I could bear it no longer.

At Emily's chamber door, I told the guard Emily's maidservant had fetched me to tell her stories and perform a few little tricks, as she was having trouble soothing her mind enough for sleep.

The guard eyed me warily, and I felt a flash of panic. What if the King was in there with her, or, worse, what if she was in his bed—not in her chamber at all? But the guard opened the door just a crack, murmuring softly to the serving maid who answered it. Shortly after, Emily arrived in her dressing gown, her hair loose and mussed, but her eyes alert. "Yes," she said, "I summoned him."

"Forgive me, my Queen." The guard gave a slight bow. "One can never be too careful."

Emily sent the servant away, held the door open for my entrance, and then closed it behind us. She crossed her arms over her chest. "Yes?"

"I just . . ." Now that she stood before me, my tongue felt thick and stupid in my mouth. Impulsively, I grasped her wrist, held her hand between mine. It felt cold, a little clammy. "I just wanted to see you. To make sure you are all right."

"I'm fine. You needn't trouble yourself."

"You look unwell," I blurted. "Ever since the wedding. Has he done something to you, the King? Does he misuse you?"

"Why does it concern you?" She pulled her hand out of mine. "The way he uses me is not so very different from the way you did. I came to your bed in return for knowledge. For my time spent in his, my family receives enough money to live comfortably, to build a bigger house, to never go to bed hungry. And my father is no longer called crazy. It's more than a fair exchange."

"But . . ." I felt a rush of heat, which I could not connect with any one emotion. "But, the transmutations." I gestured toward a spinning wheel in the corner. "He demands too much, too soon."

"He does not demand overmuch in that regard," she said. "He still believes I need recovery time after any substantial transmutation."

"But does he *love* you, Emily?" The question rushed out as if I were under a spell, as if those words somehow had life through no consent of my own.

"What does that matter? You didn't."

I had never felt smaller in my life. I wanted to say, *What good would it do me, with my broken body and my hard heart, to love someone like you?* But I said nothing. I said nothing because that was when I first knew she was wrong.

I resorted to kitchen gossip.

Trying to sound casual, I asked Gertrude, "Have you learned yet what our new Queen's favorite dishes are?" I crawled up on a stool and reached into a basket of imperfectly shaped rolls.

"Queen or no, she comes from common folk," said Gertrude, wiping her flour-covered hands on her apron. "And common folk know that when someone puts a meal before you free of money or labor, you don't complain. She eats what's prepared without a peep, and I only wish there were more like her in this place."

"Her appetite is healthy?"

"Why are you snooping out the Queen's eating habits?" Gertrude planted her hands on her hips. "When someone becomes preoccupied with what and whether royalty are eating, I get mighty suspicious."

"It's just that she's seemed ill, since the wedding. I can't be the only one who has noticed it."

"Oh, that." Gertrude laughed, the rolls of fat at her belly and under her chin jiggling. "She's got no worse affliction than any woman newly married and vigorously bedded. She's bred, I suspect. She'll look better once this first stage passes."

"With child? But already at the wedding, she was pale."

"You may play stupid for the King's coins, but don't play stupid with me," said Gertrude. "Emily wouldn't have been the first bride to give herself to the groom before the ceremony. Our King is not known for his patience."

*Had* the King been bedding Emily, even as I was? There was, of course, another possibility, but I would not dwell upon it. That child was promised to Laurus, no matter who had put it in her belly. I left my roll upon the table, half-eaten. I no longer had any appetite.

I'll say one thing about Emily's lethargic state: it made it easy to convince the guard, for a second time, that she was in need of late-night jokes and tricks. This time, he even mumbled, "Do something to make her smile again, will you? We'll all be a lot happier when she does."

Emily did not meet me at the door; she sent her maidservant to give me permission to enter, then excused her. Lit only by one lamp, the sitting room was empty. I made my way through it, then tentatively pushed open the door to the bedchamber. There was more light inside, candles lit along the walls and casting their glow throughout the room. Emily stood at the long, high eastern window. I imagined the way it must shower her with sunshine when she awoke each morning.

"Why didn't you tell me you were with child?" I bustled toward her.

She looked over her shoulder at me. Her blonde hair cascaded against the milky blue nightdress she wore. Her voice was as cool as the color of that nightdress: "Why do you think?"

I shook my head, took her hand. "That's not what I meant, Emily. I mean, it would have answered my questions, assuaged my fears about whether you were unwell."

"Answered your questions," she scoffed, turning back toward the window. "The way you answer mine?"

I traced a small circle on the polished marble floor with the toe of my shoe. "Emily, I—it's not . . ." But I couldn't finish, couldn't tell her that the reason I wanted the child wasn't important. I wouldn't lie to her like that; it was the most important thing in the world.

"Why do you want the child?"

To my annoyance, I felt a stinging in my eyes. I'd endured worse than anything Emily had ever said or done to me. So why was I practically reduced to a babe as I stood beside her? I could never tell her that giving Laurus the child now was more important than ever. Because now that I had tasted a woman's touch and could imagine what a woman's love might be like, how could I go back to a life of solitude and celibacy? She would have more children, perhaps the King's love in time, riches, a kingdom, security for her family. But if I couldn't pay Laurus's price, what could I ever have? Did I have to humiliate myself by saying it to her? Did she have to be so damn selfish?

"He won't let you do it, you know." She turned fully to face me, her hand resting protectively over her belly. "This is the *King's child*, the heir to his throne. He'll be the most protected child in the kingdom." She squared her jaw. "And I can transmute on my own now. No one will even believe you if you tell them the truth."

My gut wrenched, remembering how Laurus had disdained the contract. "We made each other promises," I said softly. "Thus far, we've kept them all, no matter how repulsive they might have seemed. You'll keep this one, too. But I will make you another: I promise, *I promise you*, Emily, that I will not let any harm come to that child."

Gertrude had been right; as the weeks and months passed, the pallor receded from the Queen's cheeks, replaced by a warm glow that pained me almost as much. The royal seamstress artfully cut and draped all of Emily's gowns to make the least of her growing belly, but the whispers and pointed fingers confirmed that the seamstress had not been entirely successful.

It seemed a lifetime separated the girl I had first met in the tower from the Emily I saw now, who could appear warm at the King's side when her subjects were watching, cool when she spoke to me, but never, never frightened or desperate. Perhaps Emily hated me for the promise I forced from her when she'd been that girl. But still, she never turned me away on all my silly excuses for visiting her late at night.

And that's when I saw the unconcealed swell of her belly beneath her nightdress. When she lay in her bed upon the sapphire-blue sheets, it looked like the moon rising over the water. I no longer approached her sexually now that she belonged to the King—although, in truth, he seemed to rarely want her in his bed, proof of his madness if ever I saw it. But she did let me touch her. It began one night when I entered to find her pacing, her hand held against the small of her back. "You should sit down and rest, my Queen," I suggested.

"The pain is worse then," she said, distracted.

Her distraction emboldened me. "Let me help you." I reached for her hand, led her back to the bed. Woodenly, she sat down, and I hopped up behind her. Bracing myself against the headboard, I alternately worked my feet and my hands against the dip in her back. When her body relaxed like hair falling loose from a braid, I was filled with joy; perhaps things did not have to remain ever-distant between us.

After I'd propped the pillows up behind her one night, I sat on the edge of the bed and watched the way the baby moved against her skin, the ripples that echoed even through the fabric of her nightdress. My fingers itched to trace those movements, to feel this strange person inside her. In those moments, as the baby distorted Emily's otherwise perfect form, I felt a kind of kinship with it, all hunched up inside her body even as I was hunched up outside of it.

Emily said, "You could see the baby whenever you wanted. You could teach him to transmute, and all those little tricks that amuse the court so much. He could grow to love you. Whatever you think you can gain by taking him away, we can find a way for you to have it here."

I took a breath, looking away. It was bad enough to hear the pleading in Emily's voice; I could not bear to see it in her eyes as well. But in my mind, all I could see were the images her promises painted—images of Emily's warm smile as I dangled a toy over the child's head, the sound of his laughter as he reached for it.

But I'd heard children's laughter, and it had never brought me joy. The laughter of children was cruel, as were the stones or the clumps of mud they threw in my direction. I'd never met a child who did not either fear me or mock me. Why would Emily's child be any different?

"Keeping the child here will not bring me the things you speak of," I said. The only thing that might bring *me* warm laughter and adoring children was the final transmutation. I left her then, so I could escape her dreams and immerse myself in my own—dreams in which Emily, with her fear and her frailty, her cool eyes, her flickers of warmth, her curved belly, was nothing but a distant memory.

The day the baby was born dawned cold, despite it being the middle of May. His presence was not announced with trumpets and proclamations. I learned of it instead when a maid, her arms laden with sheets, nearly tripped over me in the hall. "Forgive me," she said, barely looking at me. But as she continued on, I noticed a flash of red on the sheets. I rushed after her, my breath short when I asked her from whose bed those sheets had come.

"One does not speak of such things," she said.

One most certainly *did* speak of such things, and a lot more besides. Especially in the kitchen.

"Yes, the Queen will be delivered soon, if she hasn't been already," Gertrude confirmed. "The midwife was down earlier today, had me boiling water to make into raspberry tea to speed things along. Just an hour ago, I sent up some biscuits for the Queen to nibble when the ordeal is done, to calm her stomach and begin to restore her strength. We'll hear the outcome of it all soon, I expect."

I returned to my room, where I couldn't stop pacing. Every interaction with Emily had been leading up to this moment, and yet now I was unsure how to proceed. Emily was reluctant to honor her promise while the babe was still inside her; how much more so would she be once she held it in her arms? I did not want to resort to kidnapping the child.

Why had I been so fixated on learning transmutation to the exclusion of all else Laurus could teach me? Perhaps *I* could have learned how to make a magically binding agreement. But my agreement with Emily consisted of mere words—and now, like Laurus, I saw that words were flimsy and fickle things.

I had to see the child before the throngs of well-wishers and gift-bearers got to it. By then, I'd never be able to sneak away with it unnoticed. But I couldn't rely on my usual excuse of bringing the Queen cheer. What woman did not feel enough cheer simply gazing upon her child?

I was still pacing, muttering, when a knock came at my door. I opened it and recognized one of the maidservants from Emily's chamber. "What is it?"

"It's the Queen," said the girl. "She wishes to see you."

I rushed to change into my best suit, to comb down my wild tufts of hair while Emily's maidservant waited in the hall. She led me to the Queen's chambers.

I found Emily in bed, a tiny bundle nestled in her arms. She gazed upon it so intently that at first I thought she didn't even notice my entrance. But then she glanced up at the midwife who sat at her side. "Belinda, I wish to exchange a few private words with the dwarf," she said. "Please leave me for a time."

The midwife, who looked as though she could have hidden twelve babies in the bulges of her dress, frowned. "Milady, you are both still quite fragile . . ."

"Leave me." Her voice was firm. "The Queen commands it."

Belinda stood, glanced at Emily's bundle, then narrowed her eyes. As she passed me, she muttered, "It's not proper. Not at all proper."

When the door closed behind her, I bounded for her chair at the Queen's side. "Are you well? Was it a smooth delivery?"

Emily raised her eyes from the baby, and that's when I saw the tears shimmering in them. Not tears of joy, but of despair. In that moment, I was ready to rescind the promise, to accept this twisted body for life. I was not at all sure Emily's misery would make the improvements in my own life worth it.

"Is there anything you can do for him?" Emily asked.

My stomach became uneasy. "What do you mean?"

Emily gently laid the child upon her lap, then unwrapped his swaddling. The babe squirmed, whimpering. It wasn't until he lay still again that I was certain of what I saw—a shock of red hair upon his head, a crooked spine, and one leg shorter than the other.

"You are so skilled at transmutation," she whispered. "I thought perhaps you could make him look less like . . ." She met my eyes, and that was the only acknowledgement either of us gave of what we both knew: this was not the King's child.

"Human transmutation is possible," I conceded, "but I don't have the skill to do it. Not yet."

Emily's eyes clouded. But an instant later, her mouth became firm. "Then you must take him. I'm going to make arrangements for the child to be carried outside the palace under the dark of midnight. The guards at the east gate will be informed and bribed in advance. That's where you will meet Belinda, and she will hand the babe over to you."

So, it was to be this easy. The child was misshapen, and Emily was casting him out, even as my own mother had done. I cleared my throat. "Very well."

"It's the only way to save him." Emily's voice broke.

"Save him?"

She re-wrapped the child's tight swaddling. "The King wants no one to see him and suspect his seed is weak. His superstitions have driven him into a frenzy of fear. He thinks the misshapen body is a bad omen. The law decrees that his firstborn son will sit upon the throne, but Lucas can't bear for the world to see the boy's imperfections. If the baby were a girl, perhaps he'd only want her put away quietly. But he's not a girl, and so the King wishes him slaughtered."

I gasped.

"I've convinced him that God would not look kindly upon the murder of an innocent, and that doing so would only bring worse upon our heads. I've tried to tell him that the shape of the boy's body says nothing about the potential of his mind, that we can hire the best physicians, that this implies nothing about the strength of the King's seed. All my pleading has convinced him that the fault lies in my common blood. He's agreed that the child may live—but only if he is cast away from the palace, never to be spoken of again. He thinks I'm sending the babe to my family, where one of my sisters will claim him as her bastard son."

The hair that framed Emily's face was damp with sweat, her eyes swollen. In the past twelve hours, she had both delivered a child and pleaded for his life against our mad King. And in the next twelve hours, she would send that same child away forever.

"Unless . . ." She passed a hand over the child's wispy red hair, brushing it back from his forehead. There was such tenderness in her touch, in her eyes. *I was wrong,* I thought. *She doesn't care that she's given birth to a misshapen child—if it weren't for the King, she would fight me for him still.* "Unless, he's no good to you this way, either," she rushed on.

I blinked, breaking out of my thoughts. "It makes no difference to me," I said, and my voice felt as thick as the air between us, as the words neither of us said.

"You must tell me, Rumpel, what his fate will be. I don't want to send him to another who would react as the King has. You are kind, and you keep your promises, and so I believe you when you say no harm will come to him. But please, I need to know."

Kind? It wasn't a word I'd choose to describe myself; I'd certainly never heard it come from the lips of another. For that, I owed her. And so I said, "I'm taking him up the mountain. A man named Laurus, a great teacher of magic, lives there. He taught me everything I know about transmutation, and he is in need of a successor. Your son will learn transmutation, and other magic besides. He'll grow up to be very powerful."

She took a shaking breath. "Will you watch over him? Be sure he is treated well? You'll need to find him a wet nurse, someone to care for him until he's old enough to begin learning. A child is not a book, fit only for recording knowledge. A child must have care always, not only in the times that he is useful."

"My Queen, I will do all that you ask."

"Will you tell him I loved him? And that the way he looked made no difference? That to me, he was perfect, just the way he was?"

This time I only nodded, no longer trusting myself to speak. I *was* bringing him to a better life. Perhaps if he'd been a straight and perfect child, as much wouldn't be true. But now, his crookedness need not define his entire existence. By the time he was old enough to notice girls, he may have learned the final transmutation himself; he could come out the most handsome boy in the kingdom.

"Have you given him a name?"

"The King wants him cast out without one, but I couldn't abide that. So I named him Rory." She gave me a quivering smile. "It means 'Red King.'"

It is remarkably difficult to find a baby when you need one. It is also remarkably easy to walk off with one once he's in your arms. People assume he belongs there, no matter how unfit a father you look.

The city was silent and asleep as I traversed it with Rory, but even the occasional drunk stumbling out of a tavern or woman sitting at a candlelit window—perhaps waiting for her drunk to come home—didn't pay me much heed. When Rory cried, I felt certain he would wake the city, proclaiming my misdeed to all who would listen.

I ducked into an alley and fumbled in the bag the midwife had given me. She'd tied Rory to me with a sling, and I was grateful to have the use of both hands as I uncorked a jar of goat's milk, dipped a rag into it, and shoved the rag's corner into Rory's mouth just as she had shown me. The suckling silenced him—but not before a light appeared in the house nearest me. I watched the candle move from window to window. Then it was extinguished, and I was back in the dark silence with a baby.

My heartbeat slowed. Rory stretched his tiny fingers and gently squirmed against me. Inside, I felt an answering sort of squirm.

I was saving Rory, not kidnapping him. The King wanted him dead. I had nothing to feel guilty about.

And . . . the child was mine. Any fool who unwrapped his swaddling could see that. And while most folks were accustomed to seeing a child in his mother's arms, no one would demand that a father hand his own son over.

His own son.

The sick feeling wouldn't go away.


By daylight, I reached the solitude of the mountain, even after stopping twice to quiet Rory's cries. When he wasn't demanding to suckle, he was remarkably content. I thought of the way mothers rocked their babies—for I'd studied many babies since I'd learned Laurus's price—and I wondered if my walking soothed him, awkward though my gait was.

I arrived at Laurus's keep as the second day dawned. Although I was exhausted enough to fall down upon his front step, I hesitated in reaching for the knocker. As soon as the door opened, my claim on the child would disintegrate.

I shook my head. Before I ever laid eyes on Emily, before I made room for her in my bed, before she stood at the King's side and wrapped his guests' goblets with gold, this child was Laurus's.

I knocked. And then Laurus was there, looming taller than I remembered, as if he had absorbed part of the mountain while I'd been away.

He stepped aside to allow me entrance. "Well, well, well. The girl delivered after all." Laurus held out his hand.

I passed Rory to him, hoping he didn't see any hint of reluctance. This was only a bargain, one we had agreed to long ago.

Laurus held Rory in two hands as though he were weighing a transmuted gold brick. "Light," he said.

"He's only a couple days old."

"I wouldn't think he would have been such a struggle to carry up the mountain, then."

My face burned. I realized then that Laurus had been watching me as I made my ascent, as I fumbled with the bag and the jars of milk and the diapers. Watching me, but not leaving his keep to meet me, not even opening the door before I raised my weary hand to knock.

Rory's face scrunched up, and then he wailed.

I winced. "Perhaps if you hold him against your chest—"

"He'll be all right." Laurus strode to an obsidian table, laying Rory down upon it. Rory's cries echoed beneath the high ceiling. Laurus opened the blanket. "Ugly little thing, isn't he?"

Perhaps Rory would need to get used to being called ugly, as I had—but all the same, anger flared up within me. *Emily thought he was beautiful.*

"Noisy, too," commented Laurus.

"He's hungry."

Laurus pressed a bony hand over Rory's mouth. The baby's eyes widened as Laurus's closed, concentration etched onto his face. When he lifted his hand, Rory's mouth remained open; his face remained red; he kept taking those gasping breaths that fueled his scream. But no sound came.

"That's better." Laurus rubbed his temples. "I thought you said this was the Queen's child."

"He is."

"But clearly he's—" He gestured at me, then chuckled. "Oh, Rumpel, you do surprise me."

"You'll need to get him a nurse," I said. "I fed him with goat's milk and rags on the journey, but it's not enough. He needs a woman's milk."

"I can't have a woman underfoot," said Laurus. "She'd never understand my work, and she'd gossip about it the moment she left the keep. Not to mention how she'll fill his head with a woman's nonsense. I need him to remain empty and open to all that I will impart." He dropped his hand from his temples, turned his gaze to me.

"Rags dipped in goat's milk aren't enough to sustain him."

Laurus waved his hand dismissively. "It will have to be magic, then."

"What kind of magic?" I watched Rory squirm on the table, still filled with his screams even as we heard nothing.

"There are spells for endless goblets of wine, endless pots of soup. I'll adapt something so that he can suckle a rag with an endless supply of milk. Simple enough."

I thought of mothers and nurses feeding babes at their breasts, the way such feeding required holding a baby close. With this spell, this endlessly soaked rag, the child could be fed without ever being held. Just as he could cry into silence until he learned his cries meant nothing.

I didn't want to see it. I would rather remember Rory stretching sleepily on Emily's lap.

"Your price has been delivered," I said. "When will you teach me the final transmutation?"

"I won't."

The pit of my stomach dropped out. "But the agreement is magically binding—"

"The agreement states I will share with you the secrets of changing your form in exchange for a child in his first year of life. This is the first thing you should know: No one has ever successfully performed a self-transmutation. Some have tried, but the results have been ghastly. Worse than what you are now, if you can believe that. But you'll get your handsome face, Rumpelstiltskin. An incredibly skilled sorcerer can perform transmutations on other humans. I can transform you."

I glanced at Rory. Did this mean he would never be able to remake himself into an image that would be more pleasing to the world?

"If I can't do the transmutation myself, why did you spend all these years teaching me? Why didn't you just demand the baby for the final transmutation when I first appeared seven years ago?"

"The transmutation would have killed you then," said Laurus. "A great deal of magic will pass through you, and the best way to build up your tolerance for that kind of magic is to learn to perform it yourself. When you learn magic, your gift will simply refuse to respond if you demand too much of it. The fact that you continued to successfully perform ever-more-complicated transmutations showed me that your endurance was increasing quite nicely."

I thought of those three nights transmuting a roomful of straw for Emily. I had never taxed my endurance so much in all my years with Laurus. Perhaps

I was more prepared to survive this than even Laurus understood.

Thank God I had not attempted transmutation on Rory when Emily requested it.

"Or was I wrong," began Laurus, "to assume you wanted to live to enjoy your new body?"

"Of course you weren't wrong," I muttered. "When can you do it?"

"Tomorrow." Laurus gathered Rory up from the table. "Tonight, I'll work the magic to make sure he stays fed. As you drift to sleep, dream of the man you will be."

I wish I could say the memory of Rory's silent cry distressed me too much for sleep, but the trek up the mountain had so exhausted me that I thought of nothing as I fell into bed and let sleep pull me under.

A pounding on the door roused me. For a moment, I was disoriented. As the knock continued, my head began to clear. I stumbled out of bed and opened the door.

Laurus stood there, empty-handed.

"Where is Rory?" I asked, rubbing my eyes.

"He's asleep. Not that he's any of your concern now." Laurus raised an eyebrow. "Still sleeping, Rumpel? I'd expect you to be more eager. You've waited for this day for so long."

I only shrugged, my eyes upon a square of sunlight on the floor.

"Let's go to the Transmutation Hall."

Although the light streaming through every window told me morning had come, my body still felt heavy and sluggish. I was relieved when we stopped in the hall where Laurus did his grandest magic. The ceilings in the Transmutation Hall were high enough for the room to absorb any magical fallout without the light showing outside, the windows hung with dark drapes, the walls scorched by years of magical energy. He turned toward me so abruptly that his cloak swirled around him. "Have you given your new form some thought? Describe it to me, that I might do it justice."

I had given it very little thought except as a vague end to the upheaval Emily had made of my life. So I mumbled the first words that came to my mind: "Tall, straight-backed. Dark hair, dark eyes. Strong hands. Handsome."

"Simple enough. You know that an object cannot be transmuted without direct contact. You must step closer. "

I did. Laurus rolled up his sleeves and placed his hands on my shoulders, wiggling them beneath the cloth of my tunic until he touched my bare skin. His hands were as cold as marble. I thought of those hands touching Rory. I opened my mouth, but by then the air around me had begun to hum and vibrate, drowning any protest I might have made. Vaguely, I recognized this as a stronger version of the warmth and vibration I felt in my palms or fingertips when I transmuted. Laurus's hands now burned hot, and I felt sure his fingers would leave smoking brands on my shoulders. My bones ached, creaked. I cried out as my skin seemed to split open, and my head felt as though it were floating away from my body. I stumbled forward, dizzy, as if I were about to topple from a great height.

But that dizzying height was only my own stature. Laurus let go, and for the first time, I looked down upon him. He was bent double, his hands upon his knees, gasping. My body still felt stretched and aching, as though I had spent the previous day carrying boulders instead of a child up the mountain. I pressed my hand against my racing heart. That's when I noticed that my tunic hung in shreds, torn when my body had grown; my breeches reached just below my knees. I loosened the ties at my waist so I could draw in more air.

Still breathing heavily, Laurus straightened. I could meet his eyes without tilting my head back now, and their ice-blue glint startled me. An oily grin opened upon his face. "Not bad, Rumpel." He reached for a hand mirror upon the table, held it out to me.

The handsome face that stared back at me should have brought me joy. Laurus had given me a thick mass of dark hair upon my head, a healthy, ruddy complexion, hard lines and angles along my jawbone. I looked down at my open hands, large and strong—and thought instantly that such hands felt too big, clumsy, and useless when they had nothing to hold. When they still could not touch Emily, who remained the King's wife; when they could not comfort Rory as he cried.

"Well?" Laurus prompted.

"I changed my mind."

Laurus's face darkened. "Excuse me?"

"I want Rory back. If that means I forfeit this body, so be it."

Laurus narrowed his eyes. "Do you know what I've done for you, Rumpelstiltskin? Did you not see the power it drained from me? It will be a full day before I can do any magic at all, a fortnight before I can transmute a living creature. I've traded your pathetic life as a palace imp for one exploding with possibility. You can have any profession you desire, or none at all. Any woman will be happy to be in your arms and in your bed. And you've retained all the magic I've taught you. Perhaps you do not yet comprehend the many doors open to one who is both comely and powerful."

"I've spent my life dreaming of it," I said. "I know what I give up. I would rather have the child."

Laurus shrugged. "A bargain is a bargain. Besides, if you really care for the boy, wouldn't you rather give him education, the possibility of greatness?"

Laurus's cold hands. Rory's silent screams.

"He's quite fortunate that I care nothing for his ugliness," continued Laurus. "I shall train him just as well. Who else would give him as much?"

"I care nothing for his ugliness."

"Well, you wouldn't. But you understand the world's cruelty."

"His mother," I pressed, remembering the soft look in her eyes when she gazed down upon him. "His mother thought him beautiful. She said as much with her words, and even more with her eyes."

"You delude yourself. Every woman dreams of holding a perfect creature in her arms. The woman who gives birth to a misshapen thing thrusts it away, terrified that such ugliness also lurks within herself. Think of your own mother."

"Emily cares nothing for how one looks."

"Then what does she care for?"

"Something else." I ran my hand over my chin, surprised by the feeling of rough stubble rather than errant wisps of hair. Never had she called me ugly, but what she had called me when I'd taken Rory remained burned in my memory: *kind.*

She had given me her body in return for my instruction; she had given me a necklace from her departed mother, a ring from her sweetheart, and her firstborn child, all so I would keep her safe from the King, so that the kingdom might believe a mad claim he made, after he'd heard a mad claim from her father. This exchange, one thing for another, did not seem kind to me, nor any different from the agreements Laurus and I made.

So what did Emily see that made her call me kind?

"I'm waiting," said Laurus.

"She cares for what cannot be seen. Something that is inside. Something that has nothing to do with the shape of one's body."

"And so it is not for her that you take this new form?" Laurus folded his arms. "Although you say these things, I think you do not believe them."

"What if I could prove it?" Hope ignited within me. "If I could prove that she cares nothing about a man or a child's ugliness, could I take Rory back?"

Laurus tapped his chin. "You continue to intrigue me, Rumpelstiltskin. I have no interest in the silly performances you do for the King, and yet, you've entertained me, too, over the years. When you first arrived on my doorstep, the idea that such a scrawny, misshapen body could learn to channel the power needed for transmutation was laughable. I never thought you'd come up with the twelve gold coins I demanded as payment. And when I set the challenge before you to procure a child, I did not think you would ever be successful—and yet, there he is in the next room." Laurus gestured toward the door. "These new claims pique my curiosity as well." He paused. "What say you to another bargain? Return to the boy's mother in your new form—if she truly sees something 'inside,' she should recognize you just the same." Laurus's lips quirked up to one side, and I knew then that he did not believe it possible. "If she calls you by your true name, you may have the child."

"The agreement must be magically binding," I said.

"When have I ever broken my promises?" Even so, Laurus drew a long piece off a ream of ensorcelled parchment. "A shame, though, that it always has to be me who receives the grisly magical punishment." He spread the piece of parchment upon the table.

"What shall it be?" he asked, pulling out a book of sample agreements and suitable consequences. "Shall my skin burn with boils? Shall my kneecaps break? A lifetime of sleepless nights, caused by the most horrendous of nightmares?"

I suspected that Laurus might accept boils or broken kneecaps to keep Rory. "Magical impotence," I said. "If you don't uphold your end of the agreement, you'll lose your ability to command magic, not for a day, not for a fortnight, but for seven years."

"That's a little much, don't you think?"

"It's as much time as I've given you."

"Well, you don't play this game gently," he muttered. "Of course, I have terms of my own. It should go without saying that you may not speak your true name to the Queen."

"Of course."

"Nor may you speak of your shared past, of anything you have done together or talked about together. And, you may not do transmutation in her presence."

"Understood."

Although my voice was steady, as Laurus bent to write the agreement, my insides quivered. How *would* Emily know it was me if I could do none of these things?

"I'm including a magical reversion clause," said Laurus. "That means the original magic will be negated if the terms of the contract are fulfilled. Thus, the magic that has transmuted your body will evaporate, leaving you with your old form. That's how I'll know whether you've spoken true if you tell me she called you by your name. You did agree that your new body would be forfeit if you got the child back."

"Yes."

"You must come back to my keep for the babe. You have three days." Laurus penned the length of time onto the parchment before I could object.

"But it takes me a full day just to get back to Madrigan. And what if they won't let me in to see the Queen?"

"None of that is my concern." Laurus signed the agreement, then handed the quill to me.

I was so weary that I stumbled several yards down the mountain before I noticed the sun was barely peeking above the horizon.

But hadn't the sun been up when Laurus woke me? Between my transformation and drawing up the agreement, I must have been awake for at least an hour, more likely two. But my body still felt heavy with exhaustion. Just as the sunlight illuminated the path before me, the realization of what Laurus had done became clear as well.

He had roused me in the stillness of the night. He expended his magic not only on my transmutation, but on creating the illusion of morning when dawn had not yet broken. He was anxious to complete the agreement while my mind was still sleep-muddled. He must have suspected my second thoughts. I picked up my pace. Sticks snapped beneath each of my steps, which fell harder than before. My new center of balance left me unsteady, but when I looked over my shoulder, I saw that my longer legs still carried me more quickly down the mountain than I'd been able to go before. That was good—I would need every hour.

By the time I reached Madrigan, I wanted nothing more than to fall into a bed in some inn. But even though I walked down the mountain more quickly in my new body, I'd still lost most of the day. I had no time to sleep.

When I entered a tavern for a meal, heads turned in my direction. Nobody gaped or suppressed a shudder. Some let their gazes linger longer than necessary. I had transmuted my clothes to fit me better, but the journey had torn and dirtied them, and the wind had disheveled my hair. But that wasn't why they stared. I caught appreciation rather than revulsion in these strangers' eyes.

I approached the counter, placed my hands upon it to steady myself. "Give me a hearty meal to fill my belly fast," I said, "and a mug of ale."

The tavern keeper nodded and turned toward the kitchen. I remembered then that I had no money. I slipped out through the back door, as if I needed to relieve myself. I found cracked chicken bones and scraps of turkey skin on the tavern's rubbish heap in the alley, and I transmuted the bones into gold coins, the skin into a pouch to carry them. When I returned to the tavern, a barmaid was coming out of the kitchen with a tray full of steaming food. The tavern keeper pointed her toward me. Her eyes widened, and a blush crept up her cheeks. "Where would you like me to set it, sir?" She lowered her gaze.

"It matters not. There." I gestured toward an empty place at the bar. Although I wanted to disappear into the tavern's darkest corner, the bar would be the best place to hear news of the palace. She set down the tray, and I passed her a few coins. "Give these to the tavern keeper," I said. "Anything that's left after the cost of the meal and the ale, you may keep."

"You are too generous." She smiled, and I noticed that she had a dimple. Her blonde hair hung in two long braids down her back. If she let it tumble loose, would it shine with the same golden hue as Emily's did?

I could have this woman. Something akin to regret twisted in my gut. If I slept away the days Laurus had given me, I would keep this beautiful form . . .

But Rory.

I shook my head, picked up my spoon.

The tavern keeper emerged from the kitchen, holding a mug in one hand and a white towel in the other. "You're not from around here, are you?" he asked, wiping down the mug.

"No." A lie sprang to my lips: "I've been traveling almost a week. I come to pay my respects to the Queen, and to her new child."

The tavern keeper's easy expression bent into a frown. Another man at the counter turned toward me. He was twice as wide as me, with a black beard so copious it all but hid his mouth. "You sure ain't from around here. You've come a long way for nothing, sir."

I feigned surprise. "Very little news reached me on the road. Could you tell me more?"

"The Queen has been ill," said the tavern keeper. "She'll see no one, except an endless string of physicians the King has summoned. She lost the child."

Only after I left the tavern did I notice the black drapes hung in windows, the black flags flown off the posts over shop doors. The last time I had seen city-wide mourning like this was when King Lucas's father had died. Now, the city mourned the loss of Rory, the prince they would never know.

I had to see Emily. But I could not perfectly picture the robe I would need for my disguise; if I transmuted one that was not wholly accurate, I could be recognized for the impostor I was. I jingled my transmuted coin purse, satisfied that its weight would be enough to purchase a change of clothes.

I ducked into a tailor's shop. He had once measured my misshapen body, crafted the suits I wore for entertaining the King's crowds. Now he was measuring a boy who stood upon the very stool I had used. When the tailor saw me, he perked up. He dictated measurements to his apprentice, then approached me. "How may I help you, good sir?"

"I'm a traveling physician," I told him, "a specialist here to treat the Queen. My caravan was attacked by bandits, and I was left with nothing but the clothes upon my back and a few coins. I need a new robe, and quickly. Something befitting a meeting at the palace."

"I do carry fine physician's robes." He eyed me. "How tall are you? Six foot two, three?"

I nodded, trusting his ability to judge such a thing.

He disappeared into a back room, and then returned with a black cloak draped over his arm. He held it out to me. "Try this."

I dropped it over my head, and it fell to just above my ankles. The tailor scratched his chin. "Almost a bit too short. I can let out the hem—"

"This will suffice," I said, my eye on the deepening darkness outside the window.

"You'll need trousers and a tunic to wear underneath as well," he commented, "and a new pair of shoes. I know a good cobbler. His shop is closed now, but he could see you first thing in the morning—"

"The King is expecting me tonight. I can't wait that long."

The first day was almost gone.

The lights in Madrigan's windows were flickering as I left the tailor, my coin purse near empty. He had brought my attention to the need to transmute my scuffed and ragged shoes. I found a dark corner in which to do the magic, changing my coin purse to a physician's bag as well. I knew not what implements a physician carried, so I left it empty, hoping no one would ask to look inside.

When I reached the palace gates, I apologized for my late arrival. My journey had been long, I explained, but the King had ordered me to see the Queen as soon as I arrived, no matter the hour.

The guard looked me up and down, then nodded and stepped easily aside. The guards and servants I encountered on my way to Emily's room treated me with a similar lack of alarm. One of the kitchen workers even implored me to take some food and tea to recover from my journey; another servant asked if I needed a room made up so I could rest before I saw the Queen. "I would not be able to sleep soundly," I responded, "knowing the Queen is still unwell."

Were these the same palace workers who had once hardly acknowledged me in the hall, who grumbled when I snatched an extra roll from the kitchen? Was it merely the physician's robe, or was it my newly handsome face that wrought such change? How easy life could be in this form!

I recognized the young, wiry guard who led me to Emily's room, and I stopped myself short of greeting him by name. The midwife opened the door when he knocked.

"What could you need at this hour?" she demanded. "And who is this?" She leaned to the side to get a better look, and suddenly her expression dissolved into embarrassment. "Oh, I'm sorry, good sir," she said. "I thought the physician was not arriving until tomorrow."

"The King told me to see the Queen the moment I arrived," I said. "Is she awake?"

"Aye, if you could call it that." Belinda stepped aside, granting me access to the room.

Except for a few candles lit on nightstands and dressers, the bedchamber was dark. As I approached Emily's bed, first my legs trembled, then my hands. I had to steady myself; a professional would not be affected so.

"Your Grace," Belinda said softly, approaching the bed, "the physician from Yavin is here."

"I don't want to see him." Emily faced away from me, so all I saw was her matted and tangled hair, the shape of her body—strangely deflated without the fullness of pregnancy. "I'm not ill."

"It's only natural that childbirth wearies a woman," said the midwife, "but you've been abed for days. The people need to be assured that their Queen is safe and well."

"If I could just speak with Her Grace tonight," I ventured, "the examination could hold off until tomorrow."

Emily turned toward me then, sitting up. She looked neither safe nor well, the candlelight casting dark shadows beneath her eyes. Still, I thought I caught a flicker of recognition on her face.

"A physician?" Suspicion edged her voice. She reached for the candle on her bedside table and held it out to cast more light upon my face. I stood perfectly still, my blood rushing in my ears.

"Oh, I see," she said, and her face fell as she set the candle back upon the nightstand. What had she seen, in that moment before disappointment settled onto her features? *Who* had she seen?

"I do not wish to speak with you tonight," she said, falling back against her pillows. "I'm not ill."

"My Queen, the King required that I see you as soon as I arrived—"

"I will not perish overnight," she snapped. "I wish to be left alone, and to take my night's rest."

The midwife gave me an apologetic look. "Let us respect the Queen's wishes, good sir," she said. She ushered me toward the door.

"Wait," I said, catching the guard's eye in the hall. "I should warn you—bandits attacked my caravan on the way here. My physician's robes were stolen, as well as my implements. I had to buy my materials anew when I arrived in Madrigan. The bandits also have my map and my notes. It's possible that another may come dressed as a physician, claiming to be me, to gain access to the palace."

The guard straightened. "Thank you for the warning, good sir. I will alert everyone who works in the palace."

Belinda placed her hand gently upon my arm. "Oh, you poor man; you've had such a frightful time. There's no entertainment in the Great Hall this week—out of respect for the mourning, you understand—but at the very least I can find someone to take you to your room for a well-deserved rest."

The room I was given was larger and finer than the tiny tower room that had been my home for years. The sheets on the bed were made of the finest silk, the water in the basin warmed before my arrival. I washed the grime from the road off my hands, face, and feet, then collapsed into bed.

But sleep did not come easily. Emily had not recognized me. How would tomorrow, or the next day, be any different? Perhaps I was as foolish as Laurus thought. Perhaps there was nothing special about Emily, and she wouldn't look past my new body and face to the scared, crumpled man I still was inside.


When I awoke the next day, the sun was already high. A breakfast tray sat beside my bed, the porridge and rolls gone cold. I scrambled up, stumbling over my new height. After donning my physician's robes and picking up my bag, I snatched a roll and shoved it into my mouth as I rushed down the hall.

No one stopped me until I arrived at Emily's door. "I'm the physician the King called in," I said. "The Queen said she would see me today."

The guard posted at the door was different from the one who had been there last night. He eyed me warily. "There's been talk of an impostor," he said. "I won't allow anyone through this door who would harm the Queen."

"No, of course not." My heart raced. "I spoke with Queen Emily and her midwife last night," I said. "One of them would recognize me."

*Emily, you* must *recognize me. . . .*

The guard called Belinda to the door. "It's him," she said, surveying me. "Thank you for your caution." As the door closed behind us, she leaned conspiratorially toward me. "You were right. This morning another man claimed to be a physician from Yavin. Oh, he was a hunchbacked, disgusting little thing, unkempt and disheveled—I don't know how he thought he could pass for a physician. He awaits questioning in the dungeon."

I felt a pang of remorse. Belinda continued, "We mustn't speak of it to the Queen. We wouldn't want to upset her."

Belinda pulled away from me as we approached Emily's bed. "I know all about the impostor," Emily said coolly, meeting my eyes.

My face heated. "It's most troubling," I said, rubbing my chin. "I'm only grateful I got here first."

Emily's face was paler in the morning sunlight than it had been last night. Dark circles remained beneath her eyes even in the absence of the candlelight's shadows. I turned to Belinda. "I'm afraid I must ask you to leave. Some of the questions I need to ask are of a quite . . . personal nature."

The midwife frowned. "I've been with her since the birth, good sir. She's weary; there may be details I recall that she doesn't."

"No, Belinda," said Emily. "He's right. I will speak more freely, if left alone."

Belinda sighed, but she shuffled out, leaving the door open behind her.

I pulled a chair up to Emily's bed. "I'm sorry news of the impostor reached you," I said. "I was hoping not to alarm—"

"Deception does not frighten me," she responded, "and I care little whether you are the real physician or the impostor." She studied me. "I just needed to see you again."

I leaned closer to her. "Why?"

"Last night, I thought . . ." Her eyes traveled the length of my body, then rested on my face. "Never mind. Now I know it was just a trick of the darkness."

I paused. Then, considering carefully, I said, "I studied medicine under a master who said healing the heart was as important as healing the body. He said speaking your mind to a compassionate listener could often be the best medicine." As I spoke, I realized that it wasn't the touch of her body or the sexual release that I missed most from my nights with Emily, but the way she would talk to me when it was over. I'd met those stories with derision then, but I could not forget them now. "Tell me . . . what did you think you saw?"

"A lover from the past," she said. "His name was Mark. He disappeared almost two years ago."

Sickness washed through me. Of course. Her sweetheart, the fool who gave her a ring and never came back for her. I wanted to scowl, to turn away from her, all things I'd had the luxury of doing when I was ugly and didn't have to pretend.

"It was foolish, I know," continued Emily. "But I thought it was possible, that in his time away he had trained as a physician." She shook her head. "It's been a terrible week, doctor. I'm afraid I don't have my wits about me."

I took a deep breath to steady the sickness and said, "You've suffered a great loss. And it is not unusual for one loss to call to mind another." I remembered Rory's silent scream. If I didn't succeed here, we would both suffer that loss.

"The baby was malformed," she said. "The other doctors have all told me it's best he didn't live."

"What would they know of such things?"

She studied me again, narrowing her eyes. "What is your name?"

For a moment, I forgot my new form, the magical restrictions placed on me through the contract. I opened my mouth to answer, only to find that the word stuck in my throat like a swallowed bone.

"Are you all right?"

"Only weary from the journey. I did not sleep well last night."

"Nor did I." She closed her eyes. "Do you really think you can help me?"

I wanted to tell her that I could change the towel folded upon her nightstand to a heavy drape to block the window's harsh sunlight. That I could transform her hairbrush into a clean cloth to dip in the water basin and dab upon her brow. That maybe someday, I could even do for Rory's body what Laurus had done for mine. That I could, at the very least, give her news of her son.

But the words stayed strangled in my throat.

So I reached for a candlestick, and I tried to muster the energy to transmute it into a lantern. The power wouldn't flow through me. I had once transmuted an entire room full of straw into gold for this woman— three nights in a row. I had been exhausted then, but never too much to squeeze out one more transmutation. I tried for something simpler, drew a

*Rumpled* 117

coin out of the physician's bag and held it in my hand, willing it to become a stone. Nothing.

I gave an exasperated sigh. Although I had transmuted items easily outside the palace walls, I could not call up the tiniest ember of magic in Emily's presence.

"What are you trying to do?" she asked.

I opened my mouth. I couldn't answer her.

I stood, I paced.

"What's the matter with you?" pressed Emily. "Why won't you answer me?"

"I can't!" I whirled toward her. "There are certain things I cannot speak of to you."

Belinda poked her head into the room. "Is everything all right, Your Grace?"

"Yes," Emily said, waving her away. "Yes, please, leave us."

I sat down beside Emily's bed once more. My hands trembled, and I buried them in the folds of my robe. What good was this new body, if I could still do nothing for her? I was useless as a magician, useless as a doctor, useless even as a friend. "I'm sorry," I whispered.

"For what?"

"For the baby. That I can do nothing to help you."

Emily drew in her breath. Then she leaned closer to me and said, "What if I told you the baby wasn't dead?"

My eyes darted to hers. Then, remembering my ruse, I cleared my throat. "If the baby lived, I would need to examine him, of course."

Her brow crinkled in concentration. She reached for my hands, turned them over in hers. "He isn't here." Then panic flashed in her eyes, and she shook her head. "No, it's not true. I'm mad. Grief has made me mad. It's not true, he's not alive. Please, do not report what I've said to the King."

"No, Your Grace. I regard everything you say to me as confidential—"

She thrust my hands away from her. "You can't help me. Leave me. Leave me at once."

My last night in the palace. I paced the guest bedroom. I ran my hands through my hair, disgusted by how thick and soft it was. I had begun to hate this body as much as I'd hated my old one. And I had traded the most precious thing either of us had ever created, not through the magic of transmutation, but the magic of our bodies—a magic I'd never known I had until I beheld my child, and did not find him repulsive.

I dropped onto the bed, burying my face in my hands. The candle on the dresser was burning low. It would probably last the hour or two until dawn, before the dawn of the day that would make my foolish decision permanent. "I'm sorry," I said, this time to the empty room. "Rory, Emily, I'm so sorry . . ."

A knock on my door startled me. Before I could rise to answer it, the door burst open. Emily rushed in, her nightgown trailing around her feet.

"My Queen," I stammered, "you should be resting—"

"I'm not *your* Queen," she said, "not if you're from Yavin."

"I meant it as a sign of respect—"

"Why didn't you answer me before?" she demanded. She knelt beside my bed so that she could look up and meet my eyes. "*What is your name?*"

I sighed. "I could give you a hundred names, none of them the right one. And I don't want to lie to you further, my dear, dear Emily." I reached for her hand. Finally, finally I had a man's strong hand to close over her delicate one—and it made no difference. I pulled her hands to my lips, kissed them. *It is an ugly, twisted name, for an ugly, twisted body*, I thought, remembering the answer I had given her the first time she'd asked. Now, the only way she could save us would be to say it, that twisted name. "Who would you have me be?" I asked.

"Rumpelstiltskin," she whispered.

I clutched her hands, then cried out. The sound of wind rushed by me, sucking the stillness out of the night. It was as if I'd been tossed off a cliff, and then as though my body were being rent in two. My bones ached and creaked and cracked. I trembled and hunched in on myself.

My vision blurred. I swiped at my eyes—and saw the teardrops nestled on the fibers of my sleeve—a sleeve that was now so long that it covered both my hands and Emily's. My clothes hung on me as if I were a boy pretending to be a man. I would have to transmute them to fit better, or get some from my old

*Rumpled* 121

room. These would trip me all the way up the mountain—

My eyes widened. This was it. I would be returning for Rory.

Emily laughed—a short, surprised sound. "It *is* you."

"You spoke my name." I couldn't let go of her hands, even though mine were no longer perfect for them. "How did you know?"

"I've barely slept these past two nights for thinking of you, for trying to understand why you seemed so familiar. I kept going through everything over and over. All the other physicians wanted to understand why Rory was born the way he was, asking if my family had a history of deformity or ill health. You didn't seem concerned with that. Instead, you picked up objects, one after the other, the way you did when you were teaching me to transmute, when you were frustrated that no matter what you gave me, I couldn't change it. And then, when I told you about Rory being alive—you weren't surprised. I couldn't get that out of my head."

"But, the way I looked . . ."

"I've seen you change straw into gold. You've taught me that the appearance of a thing is nothing." She lowered her gaze then, but her grip on my hand tightened. "And," she said softly, "no one else has ever looked at me like you do. Not the King. Not even Mark."

I swallowed hard. My transformation was complete, but I still felt cracked down the middle. I was torn between a desire to stay with Emily as long as possible, and another to leave immediately for Rory. On the edges of both these desires floated a sadness that shamed me—the ache of knowing that, although I had won back my son, he would never see a strong or handsome man when he looked at me.

For the first time, I poured my story out to Emily. I told her how I'd wanted to be changed so badly I thought any price was worth it—and how I knew I was wrong when Rory's cries were left unheeded. "So I made a second bargain with Laurus, just as binding as the first. He promised me that if you spoke my name, I would have Rory back."

Emily's eyes shone with tears. "I knew," she whispered. "All along, I knew."

"What? Who I really was? Why I wanted the child?"

She shook her head. "That if my firstborn child was also yours, you would protect him."

Although the spell had been broken, I still found any words of reply lodged in my throat. All those nights teaching her transmutation. The way she'd so readily offered her own body as payment. Had she been desperate to learn, or just to get into my bed so we would share the firstborn child she'd promised me? "You did it all . . . to protect the child?"

"I only wish you could bring him back here," Emily said, evading my question. "I trust you to keep him safe, to raise him with kindness. Perhaps . . . perhaps you can find a way to send word, from time-to-time . . ."

"I'll have to leave Madrigan," I said. "With Laurus's transformation, I could have stayed in the city forever. But if the King ever thought of Rory when he looked upon me, he would have both our heads—and who would protect the child then?" I smiled a little. "Perhaps I'll go to Yavin."

Emily looked away, and a teardrop slid down her cheek. "I did what I did for many reasons. That doesn't make anything that happened less true. I will always remember your kindness to me, Rumpelstiltskin. And now, my debt to you is one that I will never be able to repay."

I swallowed against the strained feeling that had returned to my throat. "Set free the poor physician your guards have imprisoned, and then let us no longer speak of debts, my Queen." The candle sputtered out, but the first rays of dawn were already slipping across the floor. I slid off the bed. "Rory waits for me. I must take my leave of you."

Still kneeling, Emily was just of a height to look me in the eye. She reached for me then, pulled me to her. Her hands cupped my face, and she kissed me upon the lips the way she had that second night in the tower. This time, I did not fight the urge to melt into her. This time, I did not fight the transformation coursing through my heart.

Someday, I would tell Rory all of it. How his mother was a commoner who became a Queen, how she learned transmutation and made true her father's mad claim, how her mind stayed one step ahead of danger and how she had saved him. And I would tell him that she was the most beautiful person I had ever seen—until I met him.

As the sun warmed the world, I made my final trek up the mountain.

# *Acknowledgments and Notes*

It all started when my husband posed the question: "What if someone demanded a woman's firstborn child . . . and then that firstborn child ended up being *his* firstborn, too?" Months later, he listened to me when I outlined what that question was turning into as we took a midnight walk through a downtown playground.

Thanks to my dear friends, Katrina, Jo, Jill, Becky, Mary, and Brie, for the long-standing joke that ignited Ivan's question. Here's hoping none of you is keeping track of which of us owes firstborn children to whom!

To my writers group, Linda Olson, Jim Phillips, Marie Zhuikov, and Jenny Rae Armstrong, who read and commented on many drafts of this story, even if that meant huddling around a picnic table on a chilly April afternoon or wrestling with Skype microphones. The story is so much richer thanks to your input.

To Krystl Louwagie, for the artwork, and to Jessica Kesteloot for telling me the story of "Rumpelstiltskin" in our basement playroom when I was four. To Jenna Ingham, for always being willing to have a chat about fairy tales, and to Ashley Isaacson, for supportive comments, texts, and emails. To Jan and Steve Johnson for offering Pine Rest Cabins as a "retreat" for wrapping up this project.

And to the Teen Writing Club at the Marshall-Lyon County Library, where sizeable chunks of this were written. I miss you and hope you are still "writing on!"